OATH KEEPERS MC

By: International Bestselling Author

Sapphire Knight

Sapphire Knight

Chevelle
Copyright © 2018 by Sapphire Knight

Cover Design by CT Cover Creations
Editing by Mitzi Carroll
Format by Formatting Done Wright

WARNING

This novel includes graphic language and adult situations. It may be offensive to some readers and includes situations that may be hotspots for certain individuals. This book is intended for ages 17 and older due to some steamy spots. **This work is fictional.** The story is meant to entertain the reader and may not always be completely accurate. Any reproduction of these works without Author Sapphire Knight's written consent is pirating and will be punished to the fullest extent of the law.

This book is fiction.

Mercenary is an over the top alpha.

Chevelle is a female alpha.

This is not real.

Read for enjoyment.

ACKNOWLEDGEMENTS

My husband - I love you more than words can express. Thank you for the support you've shown me. Some days you drive me crazy, other days I just want to kiss your face off. Who knew this would turn out to be our life, but in this journey, I wouldn't want to spend it with anyone else. Thanks for falling for my brand of crazy. I love you, I'm thankful for you, I can't say it enough.

My boys - You are my whole world. I love you both. This never changes, and you better not be reading these books until you're thirty and tell yourself your momma did not write them! I can never express how grateful I am for your support. You are quick to tell me that my career makes you proud, that I make you proud. As far as mom wins go; that one takes the cake. I love you with every beat of my heart and I will forever.

My Beta Babes - Wendi Stacilaucki-Hunsicker, Lindsay Lupher, Patti West, Tara Slone, and Terina Dolezal. This wouldn't be possible without you. I can't express my gratitude enough for each of you. Thank you so much!

Editor Mitzi Carroll – You're one of the most dedicated, kindest people I've come across in this industry. Your hard work makes mine stand out, and I'm so grateful! Thank you for pouring tons of hours into my passion and being so wonderful to me. Thank you for your friendship and support.

CT Cover Creations – I cannot thank you enough for the wonderful work you've done for me. Your support truly means so much. I can't wait to see our future projects, you always blow me away. You are a creative genius!

Golden Czermak with FuriousFotog - Thank you so much for the support you've been kind enough to show me in our book community. Your talent is beyond amazing and I look forward to our future projects. You by far have the most easy to use, organized, book cover friendly website I've come across. You made the entire process quick and easy.

Model Nick Margiotta – Thank you for being a great guy to work with and a good sport about being on my cover. You capture my character perfectly. Hopefully I can meet you one day and thank you in person.

Brenda Wright with Formatting Done Wright – Thank you so much for making my books always look professional and beautiful. I truly appreciate it and the kindness you've shown me. I know I can depend on you even in short notice and it's so refreshing. You are always quick and efficient, thank you!!!

My Blogger Friends –YOU ARE AMAZING! I LOVE YOU! No really, I do!!! You take a new chance on me with each book and in return share my passion with the world. You never truly get enough credit, and I'm forever grateful!

My Readers – I love you. You make my life possible, thank you. I can't wait to meet many of you this year and in the future!

ALSO BY SAPPHIRE

Oath Keepers MC Series

Secrets
Exposed
Relinquish
Forsaken Control
Friction
Princess
Sweet Surrender – free short story
Love and Obey – free short story
Daydream
Baby
Chevelle

Russkaya Mafiya Series

Secrets
Corrupted
Corrupted Counterparts – free short story
Unwanted Sacrifices
Undercover Intentions

Dirty Down South Series

1st Time Love

3 Times the Heat

Complete Standalones

Gangster
Unexpected Forfeit
The Main Event – free short story
Oath Keepers MC Collection
Russian Roulette

COMMON MC TERMS

MC - Motorcycle Club

Ol' Lady - Significant Other

Chapel - Where Church is Held

Clubhouse/ Compound – MC home base

Church - MC 'Meeting'

Oath Keepers/Widow Makers hybrid charter:

Viking – President (Prez),

Heir to the Widow Makers MC, previous NOMAD

Blaze – Vikings cousin and Princesses security,

previous Widow Maker

Torch – Death Dealer (punisher/enforcer), previous

Widow Maker, grew up with Viking.

Chaos – Close with the NOMADS,

Ex NFL football player

Nightmare – Good friend to Viking and Exterminator,

club officer, previous NOMAD

Saint and Sinner – Hell Raisers, previous NOMADS

Smokey – Treasurer, previous Widow Maker

Odin – Vice President (VP), Vikings younger brother,

previous Widow Maker

Mercenary – Transfer from Chicago Charter

Scot – Deceased

Bronx - Deceased

NOMADS:

Exterminator

Ruger

Spider

Original Oath Keepers MC:

Ares - Prez

Cain – VP

2 Piece – Gun Runner - SAA

Twist – Unholy One

Spin – Treasurer

Snake – Previous President's son

Capone – Deceased

Smiles – Deceased

Shooter – Deceased

Scratch – Deceased

DEDICATION

To the haters.

May they get crotch rot and their dicks fall off.

PLAYLIST

Flower – Moby
Come Together – Gary Clark Jr
Zombie – The Cranberries
Dreams – The Cranberries
Thought Contagion – Muse
If You Want Love – NF
Hands Up – NF
Got You On My Mind- NF
Natural Blues – Moby
Wolves – Selena Gomez, Marshmello
Real – NF
Hash Pipe – Weezer
Till It's Gone – Yelawolf
Suit and Jacket – Judah and the Lion
You're Special – NF
Tattooed In Reverse – Marilyn Manson
I Don't Like The Drugs – Marilyn Manson
Daylight – Yelawolf
Let's Roll – Yelawolf Ft. Kid Rock
Hate Me – Blue October
Uprising – Muse
Psycho – Breaking Benjamin

Sapphire Knight

1. **She is built for a savage.**

- M.A.

MERCENARY

"Mercenary." My new Prez flicks his hard gaze over me as he takes the seat beside me.

My eyebrow hikes, but that's all. I owe fuck all to him or anybody else. You get my respect by earning it, even if everyone around this place claims you're a bad motherfucker.

"Pretty sure the perfect job for you just fell in my lap."

I grunt. If he asks me to mow out front, I'm going to have to tell him to fuck off. I doubt it since he's not a pussy. Whatever he offers, I hope it's not out in the middle of this Texas sun. I came from Chicago; I'm not used to this heat. It's like being stuck in the depths of hell outside. The others don't mind it too much, but the shit makes my skin want to shrivel up and fall off.

"Heard you know your way around a few muscle cars."

"Then you heard right." I turn my head to the side, my neck cracking with the movement.

"I've got some built up interest in a few, you could say. The bitch down at The Pit owes me a favor, and I've caught wind that a few Iron Fists have been nosin' around. This is my fuckin' turf, even where The Pit lies. I'm not trying to go to war, but I need any bit of information on these motherfuckers I can come up with."

My tongue rakes across the front of my teeth, savoring any leftover liquor before I open my mouth to think. "The fuck's The Pit?" I've already been briefed about the Iron Fists, a rival club up to no good where our colors and lives are concerned.

He smirks as his cousin Blaze sets a fresh beer down in front of him. "It's a racetrack."

"No shit?" I spent my teenage years racing old muscle cars with my father; it was the main thing we bonded over when I was growing up. Racing is in my blood the same as riding is. I can never get enough of the adrenaline, the speed, and the wind on my skin.

I'll admit, he's right about it being the perfect job for me if he wants me to drive for the club. "I don't have a car."

"Like I said, they owe me a few favors over there. They'll let you use a car, just try not to fuck it up too badly. Supposedly a few pricks wearing Fists' colors have been showing up lately to place bets. They should keep their distance from you, but if you're around Chevelle, you may hear something useful."

"All right, I can do that."

"Bet. I'll call down there, so they expect you. Ask for Chevelle. And keep your guard up; they're not the welcoming type to new faces. They'll try to ass rape you the moment they hear you can race too. I sure as fuck hope you know what you're doin' and aren't dumb enough to place high bets."

"I do. I'll keep my ears open and win some money to boot."

An amused smirk plays on his lips as if he knows something I don't. However, I know how well I drive. They don't have a fucking clue.

"How do I get there?"

"Hit the main road, hang a left. It's about thirty minutes down on your left side if you run about eighty miles an hour. I'm assuming that's not too fast for you."

I shrug and get to my feet. Obviously, he's trying to give me some shit being the new member around here, but I was in the Chicago charter since they put that bitch together. This isn't my first rodeo; they'll learn soon enough around here.

The Pit was easy enough to find. I thought it'd be some run-down dirt track off the side of the road. That's not the case though. This place is a fully enclosed old stadium. It's called The Pit because, at one time, it was a football field, and rather than having a field below, it's been replaced with a large race track. And I'm guessing with a set up like this, these aren't your backyard sports cars being raced.

Striding through the massive entry, I glance around for whoever is expecting me. There are a few guys walking around wearing blue and green STAFF shirts, but no one looking like they know who the hell I am.

"Hey, you know a Chevelle?" I holler at the dude closest to me.

His eyebrows raise, his curious gaze skirting over me from top to bottom. I get it; I look scary as fuck—been told that for years now. I think the only one not frightened when they see me is my parents. They've had years to get used to my ominous appearance.

"Thought I knew all the Oath Keepers," he comments after a second, staring at the patch with my road name.

"I just got here," I say in case he attempts to fill me full of some bullshit. Not being familiar with me, it wouldn't surprise me if he thought I was an imposter. It damn sure wouldn't be the first time randoms pop up dressed like rival club members. Normally I'd just tell him to fuck off, but the Prez needs me here, and I don't want to return from already screwing shit up. Being the black sheep of my last club was bad enough. I'm not aiming to be the same here.

"Ah." He nods. "You can find Chevelle down in the middle of The Pit, head tucked under a hood." He gestures to the opening leading to a tunnel on his right.

"Appreciate it," I reply, trekking in that direction. The building's pretty bare. It's like any other stadium with concrete and block walls. Various vendor carts not yet open for business pepper each side of the walkway. I bet this place makes a ton of money set up like this.

The cool tunnel opens up to stadium stacked seating, and I'm about halfway up. Glancing down, I take in multiple levels of stairs, all leading to the outside of the track. There's a fence surrounding it at the bottom and a few doors to enter.

Off to the far right in the back corner is an opening the size of a car bay. I'm guessing that's how the drivers get in and out.

Pretty sweet set up, but how do they filter the exhaust out in the enclosed space? Glancing up, the very middle of the dome has various mechanisms attached to it, and it hits me. Race nights, they open the damn roof. Pretty fucking awesome. Not only do you get racing, bets, and food, but also the comforts of being inside and outside all at once. Whoever Chevelle is, they're a genius turning the stadium into this.

In the very center of the circle track is a row of five classic muscle cars, so cherry they make my dick hard. They range from bright yellow, midnight, navy, ivory, maroon, and crimson — their flawless paint covered in a clear glossy topcoat that makes them look as if they were just sprayed. Whoever owns these babies doesn't fuck around and sinks a pretty penny into keeping them top-notch. I can only imagine what's under the hoods; they're a grown man's wet dream.

Skirting down each row of stairs, my calves burn from the lack of support that my broken-in black leather steel toed riding boots offer. Eventually, I wrench open a door made up of chain-link fence and head toward the vehicles. Each car has its hood raised, and I can make out someone underneath one of them.

I'm greeted with a gorgeous ass poking out from under a waxed red hood; the rest of her body's buried under the metal. "I'm looking for Chevelle," I grumble loud enough for the female to hear me. Hopefully, she knows where I can find him.

Her body stiffens before she replies, "Who?"

"Chevelle. I was told he was down here. Is he somewhere else?"

She curses but doesn't say anything else.

I watch her wiggle around, doing who knows what under there. I'm not good at being patient, and it wears thin quickly. "You know where I can find him, sweet cheeks? It's important."

Another moment passes before she scoots back and stands to her full height, meeting my gaze. She's got grease smudged above her eyebrow, and it's pretty fucking hot to see a chick not scared to get a little grease on her.

"You a cop?"

I snort. "Do I look like a cop to you?"

Her eyes land on my Oath Keeper patch and she lets out a small sigh.

"I'm not here to cause any trouble." I hold my hands up and attempt to look friendly. I'm sure my lips moving look more like a grimace than a smile, but I'm not here to make friends, so it's the best I've got at the moment.

She licks her lips. "Chevelle." She throws her hand out, eyeing me from my boots to the spikey locks on my head resembling the color of ink.

Not what I was expecting—not one fucking bit. I thought Chevelle was a nickname for a man, but the person in front of me with curves resembling the lines of the sleekest sports car is far from a man.

My paw engulfs her dainty hand, swallowing her tanned flesh up with mine, and my signature cocky smirk plays along my mouth. This bitch will be in my bed, no doubt. Shall I wager how long it'll take me to make it happen? Nah, we'll leave that up to my talents not many have the strength to resist. Women love me, and I couldn't be more grateful for having that touch bestowed upon me.

My own gaze takes her in, looking my fill before she replaces her curiosity with a snarl. A fuckin' angry kitten is what she reminds me of, and I have to bite my tongue from laughing and infuriating her further. "I was told to find you."

"Yeah?" Shutters come over her bored gaze, and she turns, striding away without giving me so much as a second to finish speaking.

"Hey, I'm talkin' to you." The growl leaves me as I storm after her, the sway of her ass is a welcome site that's for sure.

Her head dips under the hood of an ebony muscle car, wrist twisting away at a wrench.

"Want me to fix it for you?" I offer, hoping the olive branch will get her to cool her jets.

"Cute," she scowls.

"Look, I got your name from my Prez. Like I said earlier, I'm not here to cause any shit."

Chevelle

She finishes tightening whatever she's been working on, standing back to her full height. I'd peg her around five feet six or so. A full foot shorter than myself, yet she doesn't even blink, looking me over as if I'm another tool she doesn't need to worry her pretty little head over. She's mistaken.

I watch as she pulls a set of keys out of her pocket, flinging them in my direction. It takes me a moment to catch on but snatch the keys before they collide with my face. This kitten likes to scratch it seems.

My own smirk mirrors on her face. "You wanna talk?" Her brow raises, hands propped on her perfect birthing hips. "Then race me for it." She nods to the car parked behind me, and I let loose a loud, devious chuckle.

"Fuck yes. Don't get too wet watching me smoke your ass on that track." I close the hood and hop in the awaiting vehicle before she can respond.

Slamming the hood of what I now see is a Chevelle, she slides in the driver seat. She winks my way as she turns the engine over and a rumble erupts so fucking loud it vibrates my feet. Gulping down, it hits me that clearly this isn't her first race either, and from the sound of that car, she knows her shit.

She romps on it as I crank my own car's engine over and follow her to the starting line on the track in The Pit. She's stuck me in a classic Camaro. Little does she know, but it's one of my favorite models and years. She has good taste — not that I'd freely admit that to her.

I'm about to roll the passenger window up when a shrill whistle comes from my left. Glancing over, her smile's purely wicked as she holds her finger up. Swinging from that finger is her tank top, leaving her clad in a black lacey bra. My mouth drops open, and so does her shirt. With that clear message, she hits the gas, and I'm easily left in her wake.

She has fucking balls—more than many of the men I've met who gather to race like they own the track. This is her house, and she's making it clear from the start just who runs it. I've raced many times, beginning when I was damn near a kid. Having the experience, the grease and gas in your blood is almost like a disease. You can fight it, but the need is overwhelming to capture that sense of adrenaline, of dangerous peace you get when driving a car so fast you feel as if you're flying.

No matter how much experience I have, her taillights mock me. I could easily hear the power her engine thundered with, feel its very breath like a hot caress against my neck. There was no way in hell I'd win this one; she'd taunted me like a dog with a bone. Making me believe I'd have her, catch her, and show her just how big my cock was. Not today, though. She has this one in the bag, and all I can do is lick my wounds at having my ass handed to me at the one place I'm most confident—the track.

She's sitting on her hood by the time I pull up next to her. Shirt back in place, covering the gorgeous exposed flesh that I'd only gotten a brief glance of. Even more fucking beautiful than I'd initially thought. It's rare in my case that you meet an alpha female that can truly capture your attention. I like them meek and willing usually, but this chick...well, she lights a fire under my ass so hot it burns inside, and we've barely even spoken to one another.

Climbing out, I come to stand in front of her. Legs spread shoulder width apart, arms firmly crossed over my chest, brow cocked. I know she has something to say after that show of dominance. That thought has me snorting, wondering what she'd do if I bent her ass over that hood and fucked her until she begged to know my name? Doubt she's had a man in her life or bed wild enough to stand up to her, but she'll learn.

"That lap took me one minute, fourteen seconds."

I don't ask how she knows, only swallow and remain quiet, because that time is damn good.

"That's how long you have my attention," she finishes, and I breathe deeply to keep my temper under control. It's not often that I'm not the one bending people to my will. I don't like it, but I need her to hear me out. I'll take the minute.

"Viking said you have some Iron Fists around here. I want in. He wants me in."

She scoffs. "I see you know where the gas pedal is in *my* car. Do *you* have anything besides that two-wheeled machine you rode in on?"

How does she know I rode my bike? I could've driven...maybe because of the vest.

"He said you owe him."

"He said a lot, apparently. Where is he?"

"With his woman at his club, as he should be. We do his bidding. You damn well know that."

She smirks again, and I don't know if it needs to be kissed off her or smacked off at this point. She's arrogant, more so than even possibly myself. I don't know how to deal with bitches like this. I prefer it when they crave my touch, wallow in my protection. Clearly, Chevelle doesn't think she needs either. She's wrong, however. If the Fists are around, then she needs me here whether she wants to admit it or not.

"Fine." She breathes the word after a beat. "Keep the Camaro, but listen closely cupcake. You fuck up my car, I'll bust your goddamn knee caps so badly you'll never walk straight again. This is my pit. Learn the rules and play by them or get the hell out. Tell your President that my debt is paid. And you get one race, and then you pay entry fees like every other snake in this place." She slides off the hood, landing on her feet.

Cupcake...she called me a fucking cupcake.

"My name is Mercenary." It sounds positively feral, more animal than man.

"I heard you the first time," she smarts off, and before she can blink, I have her hair in my fist, her head wrenched back as I lean in.

Scenting her neck, my hard gaze set intently on hers. "Then you'd be smart to remember it." I rasp, and she cackles. With a grip on my wrist, she twists, bends, and sends me flying.

My back lands on the packed dirt and rocks knock the breath from lungs. Not often does someone get the beat on me. I'm blinking up at the sky, getting my thoughts together, willing myself not to kill her when her head pops over me. She blocks out the brightness of the industrial size lights, her hair draped around her enough to make out every single feature of her face.

"I wasn't kidding about busting out your knees. First race is Saturday night. Oh, and cupcake? Keep your hands to yourself, for your own safety."

I can't speak. I'm positively livid, and my growl gives it away easily enough. She smiles and then trots off without another word. Climbing to my feet, I glance around, thankful for the small mercy of being alone. I'd have to kill someone if they witnessed what just happened.

Instantly I seek her out, watching as she walks away. Her ass is beyond perfect, her hair nearly touching the juicy globes. Her attitude makes me want to rip someone's head off. Her smirk makes me want to implant my fist into a wall, and that body, fuck me, do I want to do things to that body.

Sapphire Knight

2. **Having a loud exhaust is like eating chips in church. Everyone looks at you in disgust, but secretly they want some too.**

- Funny Meme

MERCENARY

"How'd it go?" Odin, our clubs newest patched Vice President asks as I shut off the engine and climb off my bike. He's outside with a shiny black Doberman.

I shrug. "Fine, I guess." If a chick calling me cupcake and handing me my ass can be even called fine. "Whose dog?" I change the subject.

"This beauty belongs to Nightmare's son. I'm dog sitting while Night takes his kid and ol' lady out of town for a few days."

"Does it bite?"

"You'll be fine; just stick your hand out first. The thing about Dobermans is you have to approach them with respect. If you do, most of them won't harm you. People have the wrong impression of them."

I nod and do what he suggests, letting the dog smell me before I attempt to touch it.

"Did Chevelle give you any shit?" His smirk is telling.

"I take it you know her?" I rake a hand through my hair, frustrated with my first impression.

He nods, "Yeah, she's not one to take any shit."

"She have a man?"

He snorts. "Brother, no one can get close enough. She's more likely to punch you than kiss you. A few around here think she may prefer women."

"Nah, she definitely likes men."

His brow hikes. "No shit? You went over there once, and you already found that out?" He switches the dog leash to his other hand, following the dog's leisurely lead.

"I may have gotten in her face a bit." I shrug and scratch the dog behind its cropped ear as we walk.

He tucks his blond hair behind his ears, glancing around the compound. "Damn, I'm surprised she didn't throw a punch. The last guy I saw grab her ass at a race was drug out of there with a broken nose." His face lights up with an amused grin at the memory.

Jesus and no one thought to warn me about her beforehand? I was on good behavior; I can only imagine what she'd been like if I'd had a few beers before seeing her. I have a feeling my "me Tarzan, you Jane" usual rationale would've landed me with a broken nose as well if I'd have attempted to hike her over my shoulder. Chicks normally love that shit, but apparently, Chevelle isn't like most chicks. Sounds like she went a bit easy on me when I grabbed her hair and she body slammed me. No wonder she's the one running The Pit. She can obviously handle herself.

"She ever have anyone around in case she needs help?"

"Chevelle's not the type to be caught needing help from anyone. She's smart and cutthroat."

"Well, she owed Viking apparently."

He nods. "That happened by chance. Viking had just killed his father and taken over the Widow Makers. Being new to the area and the Oath Keepers he rode with, he wanted us to do something other than drink at the bar."

"Nothing wrong with the bar," I grumble, and he continues.

"Anyhow, we rode out to The Pit. People didn't know what to think when they saw us, two different patches rolling up together, our bikes sounding like angry thunder."

"What was the big deal?"

"Widow Makers were notorious in the south like the Iron Fists are in the west; they didn't get along with anyone. Naturally, The Pit calls to a lot of us, the speed and engines, not to mention the fresh pussy floating around and open bets."

"That'd definitely be somewhere I'd enjoy."

He nods. "Well, when you have different folks from about sixty different clubs seeing the two together, they band together to challenge you, being that most Austin clubs are on a truce with one another."

"Oh shit."

"Viking got them all to chill the fuck out. Saved The Pit from a shit ton of damage. Chevelle was called in since she runs the place. She witnessed everything, and in the end, told Viking thanks and that she owed him. Don't know what she planned on owing him since he'd had Princess at the time. Hell, half of us thought maybe he was alpha enough that she wanted to actually fuck him."

"Did he?"

He shakes his head. "Nope, nothing ever came of it. I'm guessing he waited until now to call her on it. And he wouldn't ever fuck her. He was obsessed with Princess from

34

the moment he saw her from what I've heard. He had it bad enough that he chopped a guy's head clean off for talking negatively about Princess." We stop walking, and the dog lays in the grass, rolling to expose its belly to Odin.

"Hmm."

I know I'm plenty alpha to give her what she needs. The real trouble is breaking her just enough to get my chance. I've always been up for a challenge, though, and it'll be a good distraction.

My brothers Saint and Sinner just claimed their woman, and I've been a bit taken with her ever since I showed up from Chicago. I was set on getting my chance to fuck her, but club law says I can no longer touch her since she's property. As much as I don't want to respect that rule, I have to, or those two could skin me up and bleed me dry in retaliation if they wanted to.

"Anyone break club law around here?" I ask absently, lost in the thought of my brothers' ol' lady.

He pauses from scratching the Doberman's belly to glance up at me. "What did you do?"

"Nothing." I clear my throat. "Just curious what the club did as punishment."

"I've heard you were a bit rough around the edges, we all have," Odin admits. "But that's why we believed you'd fit in with us. The last thing you want to do is cross my brother or any others, in any way."

"Is that coming from the man's blood brother or the VP of my club?"

"Both. No one knows him better than me. Well, maybe his ol' lady, but when it comes to club business, I know what makes Viking tick. He values his club and woman."

"Good to know," I reply, and he stands from his haunches.

"I won't pretend to know what you're goin' through man but trust me when I say Texas is the best place for you. Especially if you don't fit in between the lines anywhere else. We're all fucked up; every single one of us, in some way."

I've never really fit. I don't let anyone know that though. I've gotten used to being alone when it boils down to it. I'm surprised Odin picked up on that so easily. Maybe he *does* know what it's like to stand outside of the lines.

"I appreciate that, O." He may be the youngest brother around here, but he's the easiest to talk to. I'm the newest member in this chapter, so I suppose it helps to have the VP at my back too.

"Were any of the Fists around when you were at The Pit?" The dog gets back up, nose pushing through the grass, searching for bugs, I suppose.

"No, just a few employees. Looked like they were cleaning up. Chevelle was down on the track working on a handful of cars."

"Those are all hers."

"No fucking way." My eyes widen, hands resting on my hips as the dog covers its nose with soil.

He nods. "She's dead serious on that track, and she's rarely beaten." We head back toward the club, dog in tow. After a beat, he asks, "Did you challenge her?"

"You could say that."

He stops, turning to face me again. "What did you do? Viking will be pissed if you fucked up their truce."

"I should say she challenged me. I had to race her to get a chance to speak to her."

His lips turn into a grin. "Yeah? How'd that turn out for you?"

"Well, she threw her time in my face, told me I had the same amount to speak. I couldn't put up much of a fight since I rode her taillights the entire time."

Odin laughs loudly, not trying to save my pride in the slightest. "Can't say I'm surprised. Like I already said, she's serious," he declares and continues toward the door.

"Wish I'd known that prior to riding over."

He nods. "You want her attention, then you need to at least *almost* beat her on the track."

"We'll see. I have a feeling she's used to dickless pricks."

"This is going to be fun to watch. You whither her resolve down so I can tap that ass after you do all of the work."

I snort in reply, and he chuckles again crossing the threshold to the bar.

CHURCH

"Brothers, church is in session," Viking declares, slamming the gavel to the table.

It's silent enough you could hear a cricket chirp as we all await to hear what he has to say. I'm at the farthest end of the long stretch of table, being that I'm the newest here. I'm not a prospect at least. I'm a fully patched member, but as far as this club's concerned, I'm fresh meat.

He draws a deep breath in and begins, his blond brows furrowed. "As you're aware, Ruger was sent on another scouting mission. He rode out with the NOMADS yesterday and is instructed to call me the first chance he gets if he comes across any Fists. We're this close…" He holds his hand up, pinching his fingers an inch apart. "To figuring out these assholes' location."

Our Nordic-looking Prez stares hard at Nightmare's empty seat. He's missing this since he's out of town with his family. "We have to get Night some retribution for what the Iron Fists have put his family through. This wait is driving me crazy; I can only imagine what our brother is dealin' with."

Several brothers around the table second his statement and hum in agreement.

Torch sits forward. "Prez."

Viking's gaze lands on the fierce man to his right. "Go ahead, Torch." The brother's built tall and menacingly. He reminds me of the Terminator with the way his sharp glower can easily make a man uncomfortable. He gives you a dark glare, and you automatically know you're going to meet the reaper by his hand.

"My buddy came through on the explosives we wanted. We'll be ready for whenever we do discover the Fists' hiding spots. No more half-assed fire; we'll blow that bitch sky high."

"Good and the guns?"

His cousin, Blaze, covered in colorful fire tattoos with ears full of multiple small black gauges pipes up. "The Russians delivered as promised, and we have plenty at the ready. Odin helped me unload them, and they're secure in the basement bunker."

That's some of the craziest shit I've ever seen too. Viking had a bunker put in under the club's basement. Unless you know where to look, you won't find it. Any weapons that come in are stored under there in case a bomb goes off, or we're raided by the cops. He's a smart fucker.

Smokey, our club treasurer, takes a long drag of his cigarette. He speaks while exhaling a hazy cloud of smoke. "Club bank is straight. Bills are paid, brothers have money in their pockets, shit's ordered, and there's still plenty for a rainy day should the need arise."

Viking nods. "I saw the books. Good work, all of you. The runs have been paying off, and we've climbed out of owing anyone anything. We need to keep the whores happy and safe. They've been handing us a steady flow of cash."

Blaze smirks. "Whores are content. We've been keeping an eye on the johns coming through, and in return, they've all remained unharmed on our watch. Girls have been tipping us more lately too, so they must be making good money."

"Bet. Any of them mention they want out of whoring yet?"

"Nope." His cousin shakes his head. He has hair the same cornfield color as Viking and Odin, only he styles his in a faux hawk whereas the other two keep theirs long.

"Even better. Remember they always have the option to leave safely. We're security, not pimps."

We all nod. He says the same thing about it at every church session I've been to. And Blaze doesn't even work the girls anymore. Once Odin took over as VP, Blaze got tasked as Viking's ol' lady's personal security.

"Mercenary." Prez's penetrating stare lands on me next.

"Prez." I nod in acknowledgement and meet his hard stare across the table. The man never eases up, always serious and concerned with club business.

"Everything straight at The Pit?

"Yep, didn't know Chevelle was a goddamn sex kitten, though," I rasp, thinking of her tight body, and a few brothers chuckle around me. *Bastards could've warned me.*

"She's something all right," he agrees, his lips turned up just a touch in amusement. "Don't fuck it up over there. We need you in the middle of it all for recon. I want to know why the Fists are coming into our territory. They think no one's paying any attention when they couldn't be more wrong. There are too many bikers in central Texas for no one not to notice unwelcome colors riding in. They're straight-up shitbags."

"She has me racing on Saturday. Were you aware of that happening?"

One side of his mouth hikes up a bit more at the new turn of events. It's sort of a part scowl, part smirk and his gaze turns thoughtful. "Hope you didn't place any bets." He said nearly the same thing before I went, and I wrote it off as nothing, now I understand why. Chevelle plays to win.

"No bets, I raced her for her time."

"Did you even get a chance to speak then?"

Odin snorts beside him. Saint snickers and I blow out a pent-up breath. "I had a minute and fourteen seconds," I admit and the brothers all chuckle.

"Fuck." The Prez actually grins and then shakes his head. "You gotta stay on your toes with that one; watch yourself."

"I plan to." I nod, and he moves on.

"Okay, you heard Merc. So, if any of you are free Saturday, head out with him and keep an eye on the crowd since he'll be behind the wheel for a bit."

"I can go," Odin offers.

"Me too, brother," Torch offers.

"Bet," Viking approves and flicks his eyes to Blaze. "Cousin, I need you to stick close to Princess now that Odin has been patched to Vice President. I know we briefly discussed it and all."

"I promised you before I'd protect her with my life."

Prez exhales and rubs his hand over his face. "I remember. I think she's had enough time to move past any hard feelings she may have carried toward you too. It's time to be a permanent move, and she knew it would be coming soon after Odin's new patch."

"You still want me manning the bar too?"

"No, my ol' lady takes priority. She's been through enough and Odin has offered her a sense of safety when I'm not around."

He turns to Chaos. "I need you to take over handling the bar. I can ask Nightmare's ol' lady to bartend a few days a week to give you a break and also when you're sent out on a run."

"Chaos' eyebrow shoots up. "I can open beers just fine, but I don't know how to mix drinks and shit. I drank my fair share during my football days at parties and what not, but never made any of them."

"Most of us know how to fix our own; I just need you back there until I can find someone else full time. Especially cause you're the first line of defense through the main door. An enemy comes in, you take that shotgun behind the bar to their chest and ask questions later. I won't fuck around after the club was stormed once before."

"No problem, boss."

"Good, anyone else have anything to add?"

We remain quiet, and he slams the gavel again. "Do your jobs and get the fuck out of my chapel!"

3. **I stopped waiting for the light at the end of the tunnel, and lit that bitch myself.**
- BossBabe

CHEVELLE

Another Saturday has rolled around and another race in its place. The adrenaline and exhaust while racing around the track is the best type of escape I've ever found. I can just tune out and focus on driving and nothing else. It seems like whenever I'm not in my car, then someone is trying to talk to me and bother me with something. I swear it drives all these men mad around here to have a woman running The Pit.

But how can they complain if they can't even beat me? It's the way I've gotten all of my cars after all. I went into this with a busted up Chevelle. I started from the bottom and with each race, built my car up along with winning the others racing for pink slips and tuning them up as well. Yet it still doesn't seem to be enough for some of these guys to stop trying to take my place around here. They're dumb enough to realize that the only way they get my spot is if I fail to pay my loan and they take over payments with the owner.

The Pit was a shit hole the first time I showed up here. It's not the Taj Mahal by any means, but you no longer race and bust up your whip for twenty bucks. Now, buy-in alone is a cool grand, and the winner of each race walks away with five k. Some weekends we have four different races, breaking them up between Friday and Saturday, it's grown so popular.

As luck would have it, I come out with five grand nearly every Saturday. It's hard to complain when you pull in that kind of money. Sure, I dump a ton of it into buying this place, my rent's fourteen thousand a month and I have to repair my rides, but I still have enough left to live on. I have a small place here back by the offices that I use as a studio apartment, so that saves me from trying to pay for a place to sleep as well.

"Hey Chevy, you got everything set for tonight?" Ace, one of the floor guys, tilts his head with the question. He's one of the few around here who get away with calling me by that nickname. He's proved himself to be a good guy, someone I can rely on when it comes to working The Pit and doesn't give me any grief.

"As much as I can, I suppose." I shrug, polishing the hood of my fire engine red Nova I'm racing tonight. She's stacked with a badass engine to leave some amateurs in my rearview mirror. The best way to see them, in my opinion.

"I've got a hundred on you taking first tonight."

"Well then, at least your girlfriend won't be pissed at you losing money again."

He snorts and gives me the finger.

"Right back atcha, buddy!" I call as he strides away. He knows it's true. His woman was livid the last time he bet on a race and went home a few hundred dollars poorer. At least he's learned to bet on me and not some random rich asshole with a pretty sports car.

"Chevy?" A rasp like a thick warm caress comes from behind me.

I twirl around so quickly I nearly get whiplash. "It's Chevelle." I correct, and he grunts. I'm surprised to see biker boy came back. "And if I remember correctly, you're cupcake."

The side of his mouth tilts up in a cross between grimace and smirk. The man is broody as hell, and I don't even know him. Not to mention hot in that *bad boy don't fuck with me* sort of way. He's the exact type that I can't afford to get involved with either because their kind always hurts the girl in the end.

"I've knocked out teeth for less than that," he admits, and I roll my eyes. A threat from him comes off sounding more like foreplay than something to fear.

"I'm sure. Well, you're not knocking out shit here if you want a chance to stick around."

"You're taking me home tonight then?" he suggests.

"Nice try buddy, but it's not fucking happening. Ever."

He takes one step forward, and it's enough to place us nearly chest to chest. He's massive but moves like a damn cat. He licks his lips and bends closer. I swear to Christ if he touches me I'll put him on his ass again.

"Keep telling yourself that," he rasps and stands up fully. With a wink, he finishes with a growl, "Chevy."

My name on his lips has my flesh breaking out in goosebumps. The man is alpha to the fullest degree, and it calls to me like a fresh set of staggered tires on a fast car. You want to put them to work, tear them up a little and make them scream for you. I could have that man on his knees, pleading with me to let him come.

With quick strides, he heads to the end of the track where my Camaro's parked. He has Viking to thank for having a tuned car for him at the ready. I wouldn't have let just anyone borrow one of my babies, but Viking's good for his word.

Colored lights flicker across the stands as everyone rushes to their seats. I slide into the Nova and crank her over just as the speakers through The Pit blare to life. "Hands Up" by NF pours through them, signaling a race is about to begin, and people cheer.

My girl purrs toward the start line. I always get the first race. That way I can work the rest of the night. *Breathe in and out, in and out.* I chant silently to myself, watching as the three other vehicles come into line beside me. None of them are Mercenary though. He must've selected the second race. Smart move on his part too. He might actually have a fighting chance not going up against me. My Camaro's quick, but she's heavy. You have to know just how to push her to get her to respond to you.

One foot on the brake, my other presses down on the gas, smoking out my opponents as my tires squeal. The track is dry, but it's still good practice to clean your tires and warm up your engine. The rice burner beside me spins his tires, but it's nothing compared to the roar of my engine. I ease off the gas, and my eyes flick to the side just in time to catch Mercenary standing ominously, arms crossed over his chest, glare pointed in my direction.

A horn blares, and I drop it into first, my feet working the clutch and gas like my life depends on it. It does though; the money helps me survive. Without the wins, I'd be out on my ass again. The cash The Pit brings in only covers enough to pay the people working here and to maintain upkeep.

The front end jumps, the engine pushing out so much power it brings the front end off the ground for a split second. The trunks weighed down enough, so my ass end doesn't slide all over the place as I take off, but my gaze is still trained on Mercenary all the way up until I pass him by. The man doesn't blink the entire time either. It's like he's trying to get into my head, but for what? He needed to come in for his Prez, but I have nothing to do with whatever they're involved in.

And for his sake, I hope he's not trying to get me to fold. I'm one person who won't let him win on this track. There've been plenty of others who've come through with a pretty face, thinking they'd bed me and I'd let them win. Not hardly. They didn't get in my pants and they damn sure didn't get my money. I learned growing up that being soft gets you nowhere.

"How 'bout I take you to dinner?" A gravelly voice suggests coming into my office. I'm sitting behind the old oak desk—feet propped up, Converse sneakers resting on the edge.

"Hmm, how about no?" I reply smoothly, acting unruffled although his voice causes my lady parts to tingle with desire.

"I won't make you pay, little one. I won tonight, after all." He winks, and I scowl.

"You want a trophy to help stroke that ego too? The cash not enough for you?"

Mercenary grins and the change in his features is striking enough to make me draw in a stunned breath. He's gorgeous when he's not busy glaring at everything. "If stroking is on your mind, I have something big to put in your hands. Fill you right up and quench that need."

"Cute," I huff, and he plants his ass in the seat in front of me. "What do you really want?"

His ice blue gaze flicks over me. "You couldn't handle it if I was honest, so we'll settle for dinner for now."

"Not happening unless it doesn't include me, cupcake."

"You're not gonna drop that anytime soon, huh?"

"Not planning on it, no. Why, does it bother you?" I ask and smile sweetly. I love fucking with him already, and I've barely met the dude.

"Hmph," he grumbles as Ace stumbles in, wide-eyed.

"What's wrong?"

"A few guys claiming they need a word with you."

"So, what's the problem?"

His eyes flick to Mercenary, and he tilts his head toward him. "His club doesn't get along with them."

"The Oath Keepers?"

At that, Mercenary turns to face Ace, finally giving him some attention. "Who is it?"

"The Iron Fists," Ace replies in nearly a whisper.

"The fuck you got to talk to them about?" The broody biker questions me next with a glare.

I shrug. I really have no idea why they'd be demanding to speak to me. Unless maybe they bet some cash and lost it. A lot of trouble comes from that shit around here, but we need the extra money too badly to stop taking bets.

"You have to go," I tell him, and he flashes his teeth, the man's feral.

"Fuck no. They're bad news. I'm not going anywhere."

"I don't need a keeper; I got you on your back, didn't I?"

"That was different."

"Um Chevy, these guys aren't the type who wait for long," Ace interrupts.

"Goddamn it," the alpha gripes impatiently.

"Fine, if you insist on staying, cupcake, you'll have to stand in my bathroom. I don't want them seeing you in here before I even know what the hell they want. You have to be quiet. I don't want to die because of whatever beef you have between clubs."

"I'm spanking your ass for this," he grumbles as his chair slings back a bit with his quick movement to stand.

"Do us both a favor while you wait in there and hold your breath."

He shoots me one last glare before disappearing into my bathroom. He leaves the door open. I'm assuming he's behind it in case these Iron Fists poke their head in to search.

"Okay, Ace, let's get this over with. Send them in."

He nods, and I sit back, relaxed. Most of these guys will back down if they think they can't intimidate you easily. I can kick ass if needed but it's better if I conserve that fact for when I really require it. I'll admit the Iron Fists make me uneasy and having an Oath Keeper in my bathroom does bring me a touch of peace of mind. Viking and his club are good allies to have around here.

Anyone in the life dealing with gambling, racing, motorcycles, etc. knows the Iron Fists aren't good news. They're a sick and twisted outlaw motorcycle club that loves terrorizing people. I would've been just fine if they overlooked The Pit. Their money is some that I actually don't want. Wouldn't surprise me if it came with conditions or blood splatter.

Ace comes back into my office, two dudes in tow. One's burly but short, kind of what I'd think of with a modern-day gnome. He's just missing a pointy hat to cover his long, unruly, cinnamon-colored hair. The other is thinner, not too hard on the eyes, with sandy locks coming to his chin, but his club colors syphon away any attraction I might conjure up immediately.

"This is Chevelle." Ace's hand flies forward, gesturing to me still kicked back behind the desk like I deal with their type daily. I do to an extent, but not quite as notorious— usually just druggies hurting for cash or pissed off racers who lost. From what I've heard in rumors floating around, the Iron Fists are an MC that you want to stay off their radar.

Blondie's stare turns heated taking me in while the other seems bored. "Get me a beer," Auburn hair gnome orders Ace.

"You're not staying long enough for a beer," I interrupt. "Now, why are you taking up my time? I have shit to do."

That gets his attention but his buddy butts in first. "Fuck, the things I'll do to that mouth. Didn't know you were running this place or my Prez would've sent us sooner."

"Again, why are you here?" I repeat, sounding monotone and ignore his previous comment.

"Watch how you talk to us, bitch," the grouch chastises, and it takes everything inside me to remain calm. I want to kick the idiot in the balls and wash his mouth out with soap.

"You came to me, not the other way around."

"Right." The good-looking one nods and steps closer to my right side, almost around the desk. It's an intimidation tactic. In a second, the other guy will go to my left. They'll think they can box me in. "We came to you," he agrees, and I drum my fingers on my thigh, keeping my face void of emotion but my body ready to leap whenever needed.

"You could start with your names and then move to why you're standing in my office."

"That's easy." He shrugs. "Me and my brother came because our boss wants a cut."

A chuckle breaks free and they both glare, probably growing more pissed by the minute with my flippant attitude. "Why should I give you anything?" It doesn't escape my notice that they blow off the other question and skip over the names. Greedy bastards, that's for sure.

"Because we'll be taking over soon enough and anyone in business not wanting problems will pay up."

"Is that what you think? That we'll all just roll over and cough up cash for you? That this area is up for grabs?" Everyone knows who Viking and Ares are, the two motorcycle club presidents in this area and there's no way in hell they'd let someone just come right in and take over. I've heard enough employees spill rumors about the two as well as watching them with my own eyes squash down any issues when they first popped up together in The Pit.

"Stupid mouthy bitch." The one on the left nearly rounds my desk, and I stand to my feet. He seems to have a problem with his vocabulary. I should fix it for him.

Ace grows ashen. "Guys, you shouldn't get that close to Chevelle. How about you talk another time?"

"Isn't that fuckin' perfect, door boy's trying to stand up for this mouthy piece." Walnut locks nods to me and snickers. This isn't the first time someone's spoken to me with such disrespect; in fact, it happens quite often. I've learned to let the majority of it roll off because when it all boils down to it, men with small penises are not worth going to jail for.

My bathroom door widens, opening enough for a large man to fit through and out strolls Mercenary sans cut, with his chin high and sharp, eyes curious and unnervingly calm. I can't believe he thought to take it off. I'm not sure whether to be relieved or irritated with his presence. I haven't quite figured the guy out just yet. At any rate, these two jackoffs here attempting to push me around will be dumb enough to believe I have backup muscle to help me out.

"Who the fuck are you?" Burly biker gnome grumbles as Mercenary stalks around my desk to plant himself firmly between me and the asshat full of attitude.

He stands tall and imposing, arms crossed on his chest in his confident stance only making him appear bigger than before. "Boyfriend," he replies, and it takes folding my hands into fists and squeezing them harshly not to argue. Now's not the time and place to tell him to stuff his boyfriend fantasy up his ass and that it'll never happen with us.

"Tell your bitch to pay up or else we'll be the ones taking turns with her pussy."

The blond dude agrees, checking me out. "I'll take her first and then pass her around amongst my brothers." So much for him kind of being good-looking. I'd rather kick his teeth in.

"Over my dead body," Mercenary declares, and I swallow. He just threw down the gauntlet to guys like these. And with a claim like that, they'll no doubt believe he's my man now, and a stupid one at that for coming to my defense against an entire club of bikers. A regular man wouldn't stand a chance. Luckily, he has the Oath Keepers on his side.

They both lunge at the same time, and I concentrate on goldilocks while Mercenary bloody ups the other guy. We move in sync like we'd practiced it time and time again only I barely know cupcake, how can this be possible? He throws a punch, and I head-butt the biker before he registers the move. With each punch, we remain back to back until I'm able to flip my guy and get his stomach to the ground.

Mercenary must've called someone before this all began because moments later two Oath Keepers rush in. I have homeboy planted facedown on the ground, straddling his back with his arms pinned behind his back. He's spitting mad too, promising to do all types of nasty things to me when he's free. I'll sit here until my limbs give out if I have to. I learned the hard way, growing up on the streets, alone, for the most part, you don't get up too quickly.

"You all right?" Mercenary peers down at me after driving a swift kick to gnome guy's face. He's completely knocked out, bleeding all over my office floor. I nod, and his gaze remains trained on me for longer than I care for. We kicked ass together. It doesn't mean I'll be sharing a wedding cake or anything with the man.

"Hey, Chevelle." Odin grins. "I see you're still bringing men to the ground."

I smile and shrug. "Same shit, different day."

"I'm glad my brother was here in case you needed some backup."

The guy under me twists his hips. "You're so fucking dead, cunt."

"Wow, that clearly took some brain cells to come up with." I use my free hand to flick his ear. It's petty, but I get some brief joy out of pissing him off further.

"I'll cut your tongue out," he shouts, and I flick an annoyed glare at the Oath Keepers making them laugh. These idiots like to hear themselves talk way too much.

"Torch, grab this Fist for Chevelle. We need them for questioning." He casts a strange look at the guys, but I keep my mouth shut. I don't want to know what they really plan to do with them as long as they leave here and never return.

"Can you make sure they don't come back?" I chew on my cheek and ask. I hate requesting anything, but if these two return, they'll rape me or kill me—that much I can tell.

Mercenary growls, "You'll never see them again. They won't touch you."

I swallow and inhale deeply. "Thanks, cupcake." I flash him a genuine smile. I may not need a man, but it's a relief to have one around right now to deal with these two.

Torch and Odin both cast him amused glances but remain quiet. Torch draws out some thick zip ties from his back pocket and proceeds to secure the Iron Fists' wrists behind their backs, so they can only wiggle if they move. Mercenary disappears into the bathroom and returns moments later clad in his club colors looking the part of angry biker once more.

"That was smart," I comment and gesture to his vest as I get to my feet and step away from my latest victim.

"I'm big, not dumb," he comments, and I smirk, trying to smother down my smile. Clearly, I underestimated him when we met, not something that I usually let happen.

"Thank you, Odin. Give my gratitude to Viking, please."

He nods, and Mercenary's brow furrows. "I was the one who knocked the other guy out for you."

Hmm, is that a hint of jealousy? The man pouts as if I stole his candy.

"And your club has my gratitude, big guy." I flick my eyes over him and his chest puffs in response. These damn alpha males always walking around peacocking. "Besides, I submitted the other one. I would've taken down both if you weren't in my way," I finish with a cocky grin.

He growls, and Odin chuckles. "Come on, we need to get these scum in the truck before anyone notices them gone. I called Nightmare as soon as I got your text."

"This disagreement will have to wait until later," Mercenary declares in my direction. "You have a back door we can use?"

"Yeah, I'll take you to the delivery entrance. There are stairs though."

"Even better," Torch grumbles with a mischievous tilt of his lips. He grabs the burly guy by the leg and drags him behind us. Mercenary does the same with Blondie cussing up a storm, and I understand why they don't mind. These idiots will be hurting after being dragged down the stairs *and* receiving an ass whooping.

I lead with Odin, and the rest follow behind. We head down four flights of stairs before I unlock a heavy steel door. From there, the long, wide hallway takes us to the delivery entry. It's like a garage door that you open by pulling thick chains. Ace and I each grab a side, yanking the chains until the track pulls the bay door high enough for the tall bikers to easily exit. Nightmare waits with a pickup truck, and they throw the Iron Fists in the bed.

"I'll be back to check on you tomorrow," Mercenary promises. "You're here the rest of the day?" he asks Ace, and my friend nods, still quietly stunned from witnessing what went down in my office.

"Thanks, but I'll be fine."

"Fine," he copies. "Then I'll be back to check over the Camaro for next week."

I nod. "And thanks for the help up there." I gesture up in the direction of my office.

"It was better than dinner." He grins, and I roll my eyes then signal to Ace. We lower the door with all of the bikers wearing a smirk or grin pointed at me. *Nosey damn bikers.*

4. **Money may not buy happiness,**
but it's better to cry in a Lamborghini.
- PictureQuotes.com

MERCENARY

"You'll talk one way or another," Torch promises as his knuckles crunch into the man tied before us. His skull flies back with the impact, and an unpleasant groan escapes his lips yet again. He put up a good fight in the beginning, remaining silent, but Torch obviously got his death dealer patch for a reason.

"I could hit him a few times," I offer with a shrug.

"I don't want him knocked out, which seems to be your MO if we go by the scene in Chevelle's office. I need him to flip and tell me anything that has worth."

"Well, your easy hits over the past hour have barely gotten a groan out of him."

"I have other methods." He smirks with an evil glint in his eyes. "Watch them for a sec."

I nod as he leaves the club basement. It's just me and these two dipshits that attempted to rough Chevelle up. I can't believe they lunged at her. What the fuck were they planning on doing? Beat her up? Rape her? She's a woman for fuck's sake. She'd have given them hell, no doubt, but just the thought of them harming her has me biting down hard in an angry snarl.

I'm up and out of my chair in no time, sending a swift kick to the gut of the man tied up on the floor. He immediately wretches off to the side, spilling the little bile he has left in his gut. "Piece of shit, I can't wait to take your life for trying to hurt her." I kick him in his nuts next to drive my point across.

Torch returns shaking his head at me. "Hey brother, calm down. I need him alive right now. You can beat him to death soon enough if that's what you want. I don't mind sharing when it comes to killing filth."

With a huff, I take my seat again and watch as he pulls a lighter free from his jeans pocket and lights a small torch. He must've gone and retrieved it from his room. The torch flares to life, the yellow and blue flames hot and ready to do some damage. I'm beginning to understand exactly how he got his road name.

"Can you see the flame, Fist?" Torch hisses, holding the colorful flame up eye level with the biker tied to the chair.

He remains quiet. His eyes are nearly swollen closed, and you'd think if he had any type of self-preservation he'd start giving information up.

Torch's gaze briefly lands on me. "Roll his shirt sleeve up."

I do as he asks, an Iron Fist tattoo coming into view on the exposed skin.

"They all have them," he mutters to me and scoots in closer. "Speak Fist or burn."

The guy grunts but says nothing.

"Have it your way." Torch scowls and brings the flame to flesh. The skin sizzles black and smokes, it fades away to angry meat underneath as the man wails in pain. This is not your back road, high school car lighter burn dare that a ton of us experienced when we were growing up. This is just plain torture, and it smells horrendous.

My brother pulls it away as the man begins to sweat profusely, gibberish pouring from his mouth. None of it makes any sense though; it's the pleas of a man being severely burned and nothing else.

"You will tell us what we want to know, or I'll continue to burn this shitty tat off your arm. You can't ever be an Iron Fist again if there's no skin here to tat their mark where it belongs."

With a cry, the man shakes his head.

Glancing at Torch, my brow hikes. "Repercussions must be worse than this if he refuses to speak up."

"Probably." He nods and leans in, continuing to burn the entire tattoo completely off. The smell reminds me of burnt hair, the thick air making my stomach grow nauseous.

"Okay!" The injured biker finally gasps as the pain finally grows to a high enough level to get him to talk.

"It's too late for this tat," Torch responds. "But I'm sure you have a bigger one someplace else we can move on to next if needed."

He wheezes and then gags with his mutilated arm full of twisted crimson flesh. It's a burn too, so you know that shit hurts worse than a simple slice from a knife.

"Pull it the fuck together and talk or I keep going. Let's begin with your road name. Your patch says T and homeboy over there says Shaggy."

"Y-yes that's us."

"What were you doing at The Pit?"

He breathes heavily for a moment, a nasally sound coming from his busted nose. "W-went for money."

"No shit. Now, tell me why."

"'Cause we knew it was a bitch running it and we could make her pay up easily."

With a growl and a few quick movements, I plant my fist into his rib. T groans in pain and Torch sends me a frown. "She ain't a bitch," I grumble and sit back in my seat.

"Why are you in our territory?" Torch continues his list of questions.

T draws in a shaky breath, hesitating and my brother grazes T's lower arm with the heat. The man screams, "Okay, okay, okay! Fuck that hurts!" The wound oozes, and I have to glance away.

"Talk, motherfucker," I gripe, sick of smelling the charred skin. I have a feeling Torch is merely getting started, so this process needs to hurry along.

"We were sent by our Prez to scope the area out at first. See where your members hung out."

"Why?"

"Because," T hisses in pain, his jaw trembling to get the words out, "he wants you gone. His grandson is here…he wants him back…and he thinks if your club is gone…it'll be easier for him to take the other club down as well."

Torch flicks his gaze to me. I know that look. Pulling my burner cell free I send a text to Viking letting him know what T just shared with us. No one would have any idea what my text means who aren't a part of our club.

Nobody knows what we're dealing with and the Prez wants it to stay like that. Well, minus the other Oath Keeper charter down the road. I guess they're the reason this war between clubs began in the first place. We need these two Iron Fists to give us everything they've got on their club, or we'll be exactly where we started off before finding these two—nowhere.

T continues through broken gasps and wheezes, his forehead and body covered in sweat. The raunchy onion smell only adds to the disgusting stench of burnt skin. "They'll keep coming."

"To look for us or to The Pit?"

"Both."

Torch glances at me again. "Check on her. See if anyone's shown up and watch your six."

Nodding, I get to my feet, eager to make sure that Chevelle's safe.

"Send Sinner down."

"Bet," I reply and take quick strides to get some fresh air. The reprieve couldn't have come soon enough. I can handle blood, but the scent of torched flesh is fucking disgusting. How Torch came up with his method is a little nerve-wracking, but I understand how he got his road name and his death dealer patch, there's no doubt in my mind.

"I figured those two would've kept you busier for longer," Chevelle mutters, rolling out from under one of her cars. I didn't think I'd made enough noise for her to know I was even here.

Her eyes meet mine, brow raised, and she has grease speckles on her forehead that reminds me of dark freckles. "Anybody else been by looking for them?"

"I thought we bonded last night, cupcake. You can answer my question."

"You know my name, brat. Has anyone else paid you a visit?"

"No, but should I tell you since you don't like to share things with me?"

"I'm a man, I don't share."

"You'd be surprised," she replies with a cocky smirk and stands. "You don't have anything better to do?"

"You owe me dinner."

"The hell I do," Chevelle huffs and closes the hood of the car. She shoots an annoyed glare in my direction before striding away, her ass swaying deliciously with each step. The woman is going to drive me insane either with that ass or her mouth.

I'm able to easily catch up to her since my legs are longer. And damn do I want to snatch her elbow and make her listen, but I learned my lesson the first time about touching her like that. She'd lay me out all over again, and that shit pisses me the fuck off if it's not foreplay. I may let her flip me if I can bring her down to the ground with me and fuck her...otherwise, not happening.

"Hmph," I grumble. "You're lucky I'm even interested."

She whips around so fast I nearly collide with her sassy mouth. "Excuse me? Look here, cupcake, you may push others around, but not me, buddy. I don't work like everyone else. I bite back."

With an exhale, I lean close enough to touch my nose to hers, my groin tightens at the irritation in her features, and with a choppy deep grumble I ask, "The real question is *where* do you bite?"

"Ugh!" She yells, hands flying up in the air and she stomps off. Knowing I'm getting under her skin has me chuckling. There are so many things I want to do to her, maybe spank that ass to punish her for that mouth.

"I like you speechless," I call out and follow her toward her office.

"Fuck off, biker boy." She flashes me her middle finger in her wake.

"No boy here. I can whip my cock out and show you if you'd like." She's silent, but I'm able to make out another quiet huff from her, and my shoulders shake with a silent chuckle.

We get to her office, and she plops down behind her desk. She's crazy if she thinks that hunk of wood will put any distance between us. I round the large piece of furniture and prop my ass on the edge of the desk right beside her.

"What are you doing? Sit in the chair!" she orders, and I don't budge.

"I'm good right here unless you want to sit with me on my lap."

"Whatever, cupcake. Now, why are you here in my face?"

"Just stopping by to make sure no other Fists came by."

"No, it's been quiet since last night."

"Mmm." My icy gaze flicks over her, taking in the cleavage from her fitted, cotton tank. It's white and smudged with various specks of grease. This woman is a full-on gear head, and it's sexy as fuck. "Fuck, why do you have to be so stubborn? Especially looking like that."

"Me? You're the one who keeps coming around to bug me."

"I just want to fuck you and then maybe I'll leave you alone."

"Oh, I know your type, and that won't be happening."

"How about I take you for a ride?"

"We both know I drive faster, so no."

"Dinner?"

"I already ate."

"Fine." The word leaves me with a growl, and I frown. Chevelle's much more difficult than most women I deal with. You'd think it'd be a deterrent, but it just makes me want her more. This is bullshit.

"See, you can go back to your club now."

"Nah, I think I'll stick around." She wants me gone it seems, so naturally, I won't be going anywhere.

"Excuse me? And do what exactly?"

"Stare at you all day?"

"Not likely. These cheesy lines leave me as dry as the Sahara."

"Doubtful. I bet that pussy's clenching and begging to feel my fingers, then my tongue, and last but far from least, my cock."

"In that order, huh? You've thought of this?"

"Every damn day since I've laid eyes on you."

"Wow, so an entire week. Excuse me if I don't feel so special."

"You're infuriating."

"And you're welcome to leave," she argues, and I have to tuck my hands across my chest. I can feel them beginning to shake, and I just want to make her submit while I bend her ass over this desk and fuck her until she apologizes for her snarky retorts.

"Fine, if we aren't going to dinner, then do you have anything to eat?"

"Seriously? I paid up my favor to your Prez; I don't need to feed you."

"And we saved your ass last night."

"You did not, I was fine."

"The least you can do is cook me dinner."

"Keep dreaming, cupcake. I'm not a domesticated chick."

"The Pit sells food, right?"

She gazes up at me curiously. "Yeah...why? I'm not paying for my employees to come in and cook for you."

"Is the kitchen unlocked?"

She nods, biting the inside of her cheek.

"You gonna be here when I'm done?"

"Oh, no, biker boy, I'm coming with you. I'm not going to let you destroy The Pit kitchen."

With a snort, I leave her behind, heading for the main level where I'm sure the kitchen's located. She may not be domesticated, but I like to eat, and I actually do know how to cook. So what if I pretty much only know how to make pancakes and steak? It has to count for something. Not that I give two fucks what anyone thinks. Even though I've never cooked for a chick before, she doesn't need to know that small detail.

5. **I can't remember your name, but you've got the red and black '67 Chevelle with the supercharged big block right?**
- Future Wife

CHEVELLE

This gorilla-sized man is thundering around The Pit's kitchen, and he appears to be making about twenty pancakes on the flat grill. I never pegged him for the Suzy homemaker type, but even *I* have to admit it's pretty damn sexy watching a man cook breakfast for dinner.

"Fuck, this heat has me wanting to stroke out," he grumbles, wiping his brow on the sleeve of his plain black T-shirt.

"Welcome to Texas," I mutter, swinging my legs as I sit on the shiny metal prep table, watching him mix a bunch of shit and then pour circles on the enormous restaurant size cooker. "You're really going to be able to eat all of that?"

He grunts and next thing I know, he's shedding his shirt, draping it over his shoulder giving me a full view of his wide, muscular back. Only one thing shapes muscles like that. I'd bet the man can do pull-ups for days. No wonder he knocked ol' gnome out yesterday when he hit him. The man has the strength to easily dole out some punishment. Plus, he's like six feet six or somewhere around there.

"How tall are you, anyhow?"

He turns to glance at me, eyebrow cocked. "Why?"

"Uh, I was just thinking about how you knocked that guy out last night. I was trying to figure out how many pull-ups you can do and was factoring in your height."

His brow furrows. "You come off hostile, but I think it's because you're too damn smart up there in that pretty little head of yours." He uses the spatula to gesture toward my skull.

"And you're the size of an ogre. Should I assume you're all brawn and no brains?"

He shrugs, turning back to flip the flapjacks over, and mutters, "Wouldn't be the first time."

Staring at him with that comment, I realize I don't exactly hate him at this moment. He annoys me, but I think it's because he's so freaking attractive and he pushes me. Most men don't have enough balls to really take me for what I am. They scare easily. This ogre, though, not so much. Maybe because he's used to being the one who does the tormenting.

"So, how many can you do?"

"Pull-ups?"

"Yeah."

He shrugs then steps to me. "Watch the hotcakes."

"Uh, 'kay, but don't be pissed if I burn them."

"Won't be the first time I had them like that either." He shrugs and leaves me with a wink.

He stops in the doorway.

"What are you doing?" My gaze remains trapped on his every move. I can't seem to break away from staring.

"You're the one who wanted to know." He drops his shirt, turning to face me and seconds later jumps up.

There's a bar above the door, secured to the frame. It's so we can slide a top lock in place if needed. I never really understood why the previous owner had it like that.

He makes it to fifty when the pancakes are cooked, and I have them on paper plates. He's not even winded, chest coated in a light sheen of sweat. Fuck me, do I want to lick his freaking pecs. The man is ripped and just put me in my curious place pumping out fifty pull-ups without another thought. The sex we could have would be insane! Not that I plan to fuck him, but holy hell, I have to scrape my jaw off the floor at this rate.

"Not bad," I mutter and hand him his plate.

"Mm-hmm, could keep going, but I'm hungry," he grumbles, grabbing a plastic spork and the jar of peanut butter. There wasn't any syrup around, but he swore the peanut butter would be just as good if not better. I've never had it like that, so we'll see.

We sit side by side on the prep table and oh baby Jesus H. Christ do I want to lean over and just sniff him. The man's pheromones are blanketing me with his little impromptu workout and cooking session. Not only that, but he can drive. The bastard won his race last night. I almost don't know how to act around him.

He smears the peanut butter with his finger on each cake and holds it up.

"What?"

"Lick it."

"Fuck you."

"I'd offer that too, but I know you'll fight me about it."

"Jerk."

"Lick my finger."

"Not happening."

"You asked about the pull-ups, and I cooked your dinner. Now lick the peanut butter off my finger."

My stomach twists and heat pulls between my thighs at his demand. The man is sinful and infuriating all in one. He's expecting me to argue, poking at me for a fight, so to keep him guessing, I lean over, close my lips around his finger and suck. Yes, I said suck…the peanut butter off.

Sitting back up, I lick my lips and peer up at him through my lashes. His nostrils flare as he takes deep breaths, his cheeks flushed, eyes blazing with desire.

"Yummy," leaves me in a breath, and he clears his throat.

With a jerky nod, he takes a big bite and chews, staying silent. It worked and shook him off balance, just as I wanted. I dig into my own plate full of pancakes, using my finger to spread the peanut butter the same way I watched him.

When I'm finished, I go to take a bite, but he tugs my hand. I watch with bated breath as he lifts my finger to his mouth. He gently scrapes his teeth along my finger and follows it up by sucking the rest of the thick peanut spread off.

Oh, my.

I see now why his cheeks tinted. I feel my own grow warm, my nipples stiffening in response to his wet tongue on my flesh. "Delicious," he confesses, his voice choppy and gruff with need. I know because my own voice thickened after having a taste from him.

"It's really good," I admit after another bite.

He smirks and continues to chew. I should've bitten my tongue. Now he'll claim I owe him for cooking us dinner.

"So, were you guys able to get what you needed from those Iron Fists?"

He grows serious, his eyes guarded. "You need to forget about them."

"They tried to jump me; I can't just swipe it under the rug."

"You can, and you will," he orders, finishing his last pancake. He hops off and tosses his empty plate in the trash. I finish my food, and he takes my plate from me, throwing it away as well.

"Thanks."

He holds his hand out, palm up. I raise my eyebrow and hop down myself. "I haven't needed a man to help me down before, so I won't start now. We shared pancakes and got into a fight together. We aren't exchanging vows or anything."

"You can't handle letting a man be in control, can you?"

"Of me?" I scan his gorgeous body from top to bottom. His old jeans fit him in the perfect way, his heavy leather boots complementing the look nicely. "No. I don't have a problem with a man being in control as long as it's not with me. I'd end up breaking him."

He snorts. "Then you haven't had a real man."

I flick my gaze to his and admit, "Probably not. Doesn't mean I'll give you a shot though."

He grumbles, and I grin.

"Thanks for dinner, cupcake, but I have to get back to work."

"Strip. I'll work your body."

"Ha, nice try, big guy. Don't you have stuff to do for your Prez?"

Don't they ride their motorcycles around and glare at children for fun or something?

"I'm doing it."

"What?"

"Hanging around here and keeping my eye out for various people."

"I see. Well since you're not going away, how about you change the oil in the Camaro?"

"I can do that," he easily agrees, and it makes him even more attractive in my eyes.

He's a man's man. You don't come across many of those now that know how to fix cars, drive them like they stole them, grill food, ride motorcycles, and fight. His type goes all the way back to the cavemen. He's a provider and a predator, and that's fucking hot.

Most of the guys I come across are hipsters, growing a beard because it looks cool. They may as well have a vagina between their legs. They wouldn't know how to change a tire or defend themselves if you paid them to. It gets old for me, being more capable than the men I attempt to date. After a while, I just gave in, fucked them to scratch an itch, but gave up on the idea of ever finding something remotely close to love. In this life, it's thrive or perish, and I'm a fighter.

I watch as Mercenary heads in one direction and I make my way to my Nova. I raced her last night, so I was in the middle of changing out her oil and checking everything else over when Merc decided to interrupt me. My gaze on him only breaks when I slide underneath the door. I seal up the thick black plastic drip pan I used to catch the oil and push it off to the side. Then I go to work replacing the filter and twist the plug back in to the oil pan. She's good as new and ready to kick some ass again.

Now if I can shake this biker, I'll be the same.

6. **Prius - I get 50 mpg, what do *you* get?**

Camaro - Laid.

MERCENARY

"How's the girl?" Torch asks as I take a seat in the clubhouse. Rock music plays quietly in the background, drifting in from the bar.

We're sprawled out on leather ebony couches positioned in a square around a low, polished wood table. Nearly everyone's chilling over here, so I figured what the hell. I'm already the newest member of this charter — practically an outsider and I need to break through that label. Chicago was my home, but I can never go back unless I want to find my head cut off by the damn mob.

I'm determined to make Texas a place for me; otherwise, I'll have to go out on my own. You know what it's like to be a lone rider? It sucks because you have fuck all to watch your back and shit to make money on. Most lone riders don't survive unless they're a paid killer. I don't have any strife with killing; I just want to have the decision on who I'm killing, so the paid hitman option isn't for me either.

I grunt in response to Torch's question.

"Any more Iron Fists show up or sniff around?" Viking's gaze falls to me.

"None that I've come across, Prez. It's pretty quiet around there when there aren't any races going on."

He nods and sips his whiskey.

"Chevelle let you take her out yet?" Odin asks with an amused grin.

I answer with a glower, and he hoots out a loud laugh. "Told you, brother. She's got that pussy locked up *tight*." The resemblance between him and Viking is a bit unnerving. You'd almost think O is the Prez's son rather than his younger brother. Both of them are tall with blond hair and Nordic tattoos covering them in various spots. Odin has less, but I'm sure it won't be that way for much longer.

Saint snickers, always looking to stir up a little drama from what I've seen so far. "How about we place a few bets if our new brother can even get into her pants."

"I've got fifty bucks on two months," Chaos calls from the bar. We must be loud for him to hear us over the low music and being in another room. He's the oldest brother around here and an ex pro football player. I couldn't believe it when he rolled up to get me in Chicago, and I came face to face with an NFL star clad in an Oath Keepers vest. I'm sure he has one hell of a story to bring him to an MC.

Sinner scoffs, his charcoal eyes staring down Saint. The two of them are near opposites, one with dark features, black hair, and stormy irises; the other one light, with ashy-blond hair and gray irises that appear nearly clear. "No way in hell he's that patient. I give him three weeks or else I say he gives up. I'd put fifty on it."

Hearing him and Saint on this is like sandpaper. Those two recently laid claim to the first woman I was interested in when I got here. Jude's beautiful, young, and somewhat innocent; she's a man's wet dream. Chevelle catching my attention is a good thing to distract me from Jude alone, or it could stir up shit with the brothers.

Odin pipes up again. "I don't know. He's persistent, more than any of you fuckers. I've got fifty on a week."

"No fucking way," Viking grumbles. "Chevelle is stubborn as hell. I say five weeks."

I scoff as Prez's woman, Princess, comes up to sit on his lap. "Chevelle?" she asks, smitten and territorial staring at the Nordic Viking looking man she has wrapped around her finger.

"She runs The Pit," I supply.

"Oh." She nods and beams a perfect bright white smile in my direction. "Yeah, she's a tough cookie; I've got fifty it takes you four weeks."

I nearly sputter in surprise. I can't believe she's betting with these assholes.

"I'll take three weeks," Blaze cuts in.

"What the hell? You have no faith in a brother?" I grumble and a few chuckle.

The Prez shakes his head. "Just be glad Ruger isn't here, or you'd have some competition. You got a bet, Night?" He turns to Nightmare, back from his mini vacation with his ol' lady and son. He helped pick up the Fists from The Pit, but I haven't seen him since then.

"Daydream?" He flicks his dark gaze to his woman, seeking her input. Not only is she his ol' lady, but she's Princess' best friend as well.

"We don't know if she even likes him." She winks. I've heard about how Nightmare had to fight with his Daydream, also known as Bethany, to get her to finally admit she wanted him.

He hums in agreement. "We've got fifty on it never happens." He smirks, and brothers around him grin.

"I'll prove you all wrong, and when it happens, I get fifty bucks from each of you."

"Done." Prez agrees, and Blaze shakes his head at us, catching snippets of our conversation as he carries various cases, helping Chaos restock the bar.

It's just another day belonging to an MC. People hear all the crazy horror stories about us because we're a bit rougher around the edges than most, but what they tend to leave out is days like today. We're normal people who like to razz each other and talk shit. In that same respect, I won't think twice to help them bury a body. Does that make us better friends to have? I'd like to think so.

"What time frame are you thinking, brother?" Odin asks.

"It can happen any day." I shrug nonchalantly, and the guys holler in disagreement. Our ribbing is broken up by the club phone ringing. We quiet down once we catch wind of Chaos telling the caller on the other end to calm down, make sure the doors are locked, and that someone would be right over.

He pops his head into the room we're in and gestures for Prez. Each of us stares as Viking listens to him, huffing at parts and eventually heads back over to us.

"Prez?" Torch's brow furrows.

"You're not going to believe this shit," he begins, running his hand over his face exasperated and meets my gaze. "Mercenary, you need to head back to The Pit. You were there yesterday, right?"

I nod.

"Well someone must be watching you because Chevelle said when she looked outside a biker was sitting out front, looking like he's waiting for something."

"That was her?"

He nods.

"Is she all right?"

He nods again. "Yeah, but apparently the dipshit hasn't left his post since she first saw him out there. It's been hours according to her. She didn't want to call but recognized the familiar colors on his vest as Iron Fist."

"Fuck! They're like cockroaches," Odin grumbles and shakes his head.

"Mercenary, I want you to head back over and stay the night. I need to know first thing if anymore pop up. Torch and O, you two ride with him in case anyone's paying attention. Take the back road and go inside through the loading dock. Chevelle will be waiting for you there, and you can hide your bike inside. Odin and Torch, you two can come back to wait for word from Merc. I don't want Chevelle there alone in case this asshole tries to break in. She's a feisty bitch who knows her shit, but it only takes a second for a gunshot to hit someone and change everything."

I couldn't agree more. She can defend herself, but if someone shoots her ass, she won't be strong enough to subdue them like she normally would. She's tiny and uses momentum to make her moves, where as if one of us gets shot first it takes more to knock us down since we're huge and built differently.

"She won't like me being there to protect her."

"I know that, but Chevelle is also aware that I don't give a shit what anyone else thinks. She'll let you stick around because she cares about The Pit too much to let the Fists take it from her."

"And if more show up?"

"You call or text us immediately, and I'll send backup."

"Bet," I agree and down the rest of the cold beer in my hand. I'll sweat the one beer out before I get ten minutes down the road, so I'm not worried. Hell, as shitty as it is to drive drunk, if Chevelle needed me and I'd had ten beers, I'd still go. I'd have to drive a hell of a lot slower, but I'd make it eventually. I won't let any of these assholes harm her.

I don't know when that feeling of protectiveness planted itself in me so deep, but it's there now, and it has my insides twisting with the need for me to get there and make sure she's okay. If I had to guess when it happened, I'd say probably when those Fists lunged at her in her office; it was like a barrier for me was crossed. I've seen someone want to actually hurt her and that's a hard limit for me. She's a bitch to most, but no one deserves to be physically harmed because they have a damn attitude and they appear weaker than you. The woman's going to end up being the death of me, I can sense it.

"You have everything you need?" Vike asks as I get to my feet, Torch and Odin mirroring my movements.

"I'm going to grab my Glock and an extra clip; otherwise I'm good to roll."

"Ride safe, brothers," he replies, and fist bumps the three of us. The others repeat his words, and then I'm hurrying to get my shit and load up.

Chevelle barely tolerated me in her space yesterday, and that was with me helping her perform maintenance on her cars. Not that I enjoy doing free labor, but if it keeps her calm and I can help her out, then hopefully she has something else to keep us busy with today as well.

I'm throwing my leg over my seat loading up on my bike when Odin rolls his over to mine. "We ride for ten then hang a left on old road one-nineteen. It swings right behind The Pit. Homeboy out front will hear our bikes, but hopefully, he won't realize they're coming from the back side since the dome's so damn big."

"Got it."

"We'll wait until you're in the bay and then pop smoke back to the compound."

"Appreciate it."

He nods and walks his motorcycle a few steps then cranks her on. Torch and I follow suit, our engines purring to life and then we're on our way, the wind and road calling to us like an old friend.

Chevelle's waiting for me as promised, and when I arrive, she pulls the bay door up, closing and locking it after I've walked my motorcycle inside. "'Sup Chevy," I greet with a wink.

She snorts and rolls her eyes. "Real nice, cupcake, and you haven't earned the right to call me that."

"But Ace has?" I ask and kick my kickstand in place, letting my bike rest on the stand as I follow her down the hallway to the staircase. It pisses me off inside that she lets him give her a nickname and I can't use it as well. I've been a bit of the jealous type in the past when it comes to women. Not obsessive, but I like to know the whys and facts when it comes to a chick I'm interested in. If they can't give me answers, then it raises red flags.

"Ace has stuck around through my shit since I took over here."

"And you haven't fucked him?"

She sends me a pissed off glare. "Not that it's any of your business, but no."

"Not your type?"

"What's with all of the questions?"

I shrug. "Just figuring out what makes you tick and weed out any possible competition."

"How do you know I'd give you a chance if there wasn't anyone else in the picture?"

The craving to touch her is too great, that when she opens the door leading out of the hall, I cage her in with my arms on each side of her body. I don't come in contact with her skin though. I learned the first time if you don't give her any warning, she'll flip you.

With a gruff rasp, my gaze lands on her mouth. "You forget I had that mouth around my finger yesterday." I'd like to have it on my cock next.

"And?"

"If there wasn't a trace of attraction to me, you never would've done it. You're not used to dealing with men on your level. I'm right up there with you, and I know what I'm doing. If I want something, I get it."

"And that's why you don't have a chance, biker. I'm not a thing to possess." With that, she ducks under my arm and continues on.

I grab her hand, light enough to get her to spin my way, eyebrow cocked, and I get to finish my thought. "Trust me; I know you're not a thing. You're a woman—one who should be worshiped."

She swallows, her eyes widening for a moment before she brushes it off with a laugh. She turns away, and I let go of her hand to keep following. She a strong woman no doubt, but she reminds me a lot of a scared animal, attacking when she's cornered. With every fiber of my being, I want to take control of her, own her, but she won't let me if I go full steam ahead, so I'll be smart about it. I'll make her believe that she's coming to me all on her own, but every move I make will be put in place to get her exactly where I want her.

Owned. By me.

7. **Women are like tea bags.**
You never know how strong they
are until they're in hot water.
- Eleanor Roosevelt

CHEVELLE

The week flew by in no time it seemed with Mercenary here to keep me company, and not that I would admit it to him, but having him around made me feel a little safer after the run-in last weekend. It's Saturday once again and normally the night I'm most excited for, but part of me is wondering if more Iron Fists will show up again. I shouldn't be concentrating on the bikers but on racing. I can't help the nag at the back of my mind though.

The Oath Keepers sent Torch and Odin again to watch from the stands while Mercenary races. I don't think any of the other drivers realize who Mercenary is which is exactly what Viking wants from what I understand. I doubt Mercenary will find out anything from the other drivers, but if he's racing, then no one will think twice about him being around and down in the race area. They seem to have random ears placed everywhere.

"There's still time for you to change to my race." I goad him on, looking to get a rise out of the big beautiful man as I head for my car.

"I'd hate to beat you and take your spot."

"Keep telling yourself that," I argue, and he grins. That small smile has had my core soaked for him all week—aching to feel his touch. I tell him to get a life and attempt to play it cool, but in reality, he has my head spinning for him. Sexually charged atmosphere would be an understatement how my apartment feels having him in my space and so close.

"You can have the first race, I'll take the second. It can be our thing each week." He winks, and I roll my eyes. "Kind of like peanut butter on our fingers."

I wave him off. Folding into my seat, I close the door, encompassing me in brief silence. The car drowns out the music blaring through The Pit's speakers. Everyone knows that, and the flashing lights mean it's nearly race time.

Running my hand lovingly across the old Nova's dash, I turn the ignition, and she flares to life with a sexy rumble. I line up, getting ready to race and wait for the other three to follow suit. I'm minding my business, taking deep breaths when another engine roars to life. A winding, high-pitched squeal briefly takes its place. The distraction has everyone's attention, and then right before my eyes, the car in question blows up. There's a massive boom and then screaming as people in the stands rush toward the exits. It's chaotic, and instantly my heart is thrumming so quickly, it feels as if it's going to leap out of my chest. My stomach twists with worry, my throat constricting as people rush everywhere.

I scan the entire arena and watch as Mercenary sprints for me. I'm the only one who's made it to the line so far, and I turn my car off quickly to hop out.

"You okay?" he thunders, gaze filled with uneasiness. He stops in front of me, his hands falling on my shoulders as he looks me over—concerned.

I nod, my heart still beating a million miles per hour. "I'm fine; so is the Nova." I gesture to the shiny vehicle, and his brow furrows more, glancing behind at the vehicle.

"I didn't ask about the car, Chevelle. I want to know if you're okay—*you*."

"I know, I meant when I started it, it sounded fine too. There was that squeal then the bomb and, well, mine was fine." I'm rambling, my brain scrambled on what I should be doing—pulling me in a hundred directions all at once.

"Good."

"What do we do? Call the fire department? How did this happen?"

"We just stay here and wait for my brothers to make it to us. They've already texted the club, so they know what's going down if we need some backup."

"I have to check on the other driver. The hood blew off with the explosion. I can't believe it blew up like that...that could've been me."

"I know, I saw it all happen. The other driver got out. I watched him run to the side and then I was coming to make sure you were safe."

"Thank God." I pant, my hand still on my chest, feeling as if I'm going to have a heart attack. "You could've been hurt, what if it was me?"

"I'm fine; I had to get to you in case your car went off next. You're okay, you got out, he got out, everyone is fine."

My fist flies into his chest. "You idiot! You could've been killed if my car had blown!" His gaze grows tense, and he yanks me into his chest, wrapping his arms around me. I should fight him. I don't need him to comfort me. I don't need a man for anything. Ignoring those thoughts, I stay rooted, leaning into him until Torch and Odin find us. I don't know what I'm more freaked out about, that I could've just exploded in my car or the fact that he could've been killed coming after me like that.

"You two all right?" Odin asks, and I feel Mercenary move as he nods and replies.

"Yeah, brother." His voice is gruffer than usual, his muscles tense. "The fuck was that?"

"We don't know. Scared the shit out of us too. Viking is calling the sheriff to give him a heads-up that we're here."

"Should I be worried about getting arrested? Will The Pit get shut down?"

He shakes his head. "Nah, Vike is cool with him. The sheriff will bring a few deputies with him that he has under his thumb. Not that any of this is our fault, but it's always a plus to have the cops with you instead of against you."

I step out of Mercenary's hold, my body stiff as the guys stare me down as if I'm going to break. I may be caught off guard and worried, but I can still take care of myself. "I need to check on all the employees, make sure no one was injured."

Mercenary huffs and his hands fold over his chest causing his biceps to bulge massively. "Have Ace do it. I want you close in case this was only the first bomb of many."

"You think because you're big and hot and bossy that you can just come in here and take control of things?"

He nods. He freaking admits it! "You think I'm hot?" he asks, and I snort.

"Cocky ass," I grumble and shake my head, then pull my cell free, sending a text to Ace.

Me: Check on the employees and lock the business doors. Once everyone is out, leave only one front entry open.

Ace: Okay, boss.

Me: And Ace?

Ace: Yeah?

Me: Be careful.

Ace: Will do. You too, Chevy.

"He's checking it out and locking the business doors. I told him to leave one business entry open for the police."

"Good, also let the cops check over the other cars before you let the drivers go."

I nod. It's sound advice even if I'm not the one calling all the shots at the moment. I'm glad Mercenary's here to do it though. I'm feeling scatterbrained, and he's a calm force if not bossy like myself.

"Uh, Chevelle?" Another racer treks toward us carrying a paper in one hand.

"Are you guys okay?" I ask, peering behind him at the others waiting off to the side, away from the cars. I can't believe this happened and that any of them could've been seriously injured. We have rules in place to keep them safe on the track, and then something like this happens.

"We're fine, but I found this tucked into the passenger window of the car that blew up. I don't know if it was for the driver or you or..." He trails off, and I take the paper, flipping it open so Mercenary can read it over my shoulder.

Pay up, get out or die, bitch.

"Are you fucking kidding me with this shit?" The massive man behind me thunders as he reads the note. "O, Torch, check this shit out."

I hand the note to Odin. He gives it to Torch nearly immediately and pulls his phone out. I overhear him talk to Viking, telling him in detail what happened and what the note says.

"Thank you, Jake." I acknowledge him by name, grateful. "Once the cops come and clear the cars, everyone can leave. I'm sorry about this. Everyone will have a credit for whenever they're ready to race again."

"I'm just glad no one got hurt. This isn't your fault. We know you'd never let someone do this intentionally." He waves me off and heads for his girlfriend standing with the other drivers.

Mercenary draws me back into his arms, his finger going under my chin and lifting it until I meet his intense stare. "I'll figure this out, I promise. I won't let you get hurt."

I swallow a bit roughly at his intensity. "It's not your responsibility," I argue. "The Pit is mine; it's my fault we didn't inspect prior to lining up."

"Bullshit. You shouldn't have to worry about this shit. I should've stayed last night, so I was here this morning. I would've known if someone got to the cars had I been here to watch."

"You think that's when whoever was here?"

"I think it was when the drivers pulled their cars in and went to lunch most likely. It was the only time the vehicles were in here unmonitored by someone."

He has a good point. The drivers have an option to come in early. They can park their vehicles to do prerace maintenance and use The Pit tools for free. It's become more popular these last few months as the tools have gotten better and better thanks to the increase in sales over the past six months.

"I'll figure this out," he promises, and I lick my lips, unsure how to respond. Men have made me false promises before, but I want to believe this one coming from him.

"It's okay, really." My life is easier when men aren't involved.

"I don't want you to feel unsafe," he growls.

I swear he's more stubborn than I am.

"I'm fine."

"You will be, I'm not going anywhere from now on. Those Fists think they can threaten you, they'll have to get through me first."

"What are you talking about?"

"I'm staying from now on."

"The night?"

"Yep."

"No." I shake my head, and the cops finally show up with a group of firemen in tow.

"You relax; we'll speak to the police." He plants a kiss on my forehead, and I'm so shocked with his bossiness and the arrival of the police that I let him without any complaint.

He leads me to a metal folding chair next to the other racers. "Jake, bring her a bottled water," he orders, and I swallow, crossing my arms over my chest. "Sit, sweetie, and catch your breath, let me handle this for you. Let me take care of you."

And then he walks away. I sit in the hard metal chair watching his ass, damn near smitten at how he's trying to handle everything without ruffling my feathers. A piece of me wants to jump up and argue with him until I'm blue in the face, but I have no idea what to even say to the cops. They'll run my name and social security number and come back with my record. Hell, I could even have a warrant I'd forgotten about from when I was on the streets, so having Mercenary here as a buffer is kind of nice if I'm honest with myself Not sure how I feel about him planning to stick around and stay the night though. I might have to fight with him on that.

To say I'm stunned is an understatement. I was expecting her to knock my ass out and tell me to fuck off when I had her sit down so I could speak to the cops with my brothers. She doesn't need to worry her pretty little head with shit, especially when it comes to the Iron Fists. That's our problem to deal with. I'll probably get some lip from her later, not that I'll mind any. Arguing with her is like foreplay between us. I can't seem to get enough of her sassy mouth and strong will.

"Have you found anything else?" the cop in front of me asks Odin. He must be familiar with the way the club works as he didn't even attempt to speak to me or ask Torch questions but went straight to Odin. He's the VP so naturally, he'd be the one to handle whatever information the club wants to share with the local law enforcement.

"No, we'd appreciate it if your guys or the firefighters would check out the other vehicles, so the drivers can head on home."

"Yeah, I'd like to do a search of the premises as well."

"The Pit owner has the employees checking out the building. The owner would prefer to pass on a formal search. Unless you have a warrant with you, that is."

"Fine, fine, Odin. I know your older brother will have his own ideas on how to handle this. I'll step back for now, but if any other buildings begin to blow up or bodies surface, I'll be jumping in with both feet."

"We appreciate that, sir." Odin complies, and the two men shake hands. The cop nods to Torch and then rakes his gaze over every inch of me. It feels damn near like a caress, and I have to wonder if the cop has a thing for men or bikers in general.

"New member?" His stare meets Odin's.

"Yeah, transfer. He's a quiet one."

"Good, we like the quiet bikers." He gazes back at me. "They know how to please us."

Torch clears his throat and the cop strides toward the waiting group of firefighters.

Odin grins. "Looks like you have an admirer. Maybe you should give up on Chevelle."

"Fuck you," I grumble and sigh. "That cop would shit his pants if he ran my license and caught wind of the trouble I've stirred up."

"I'm sure he'd find a way to punish you." He snickers, and I glower at his and Torch's grinning faces.

"That's not my idea of a good time. Now, what are we going to do about that note? You didn't want the cop to see it?" Odin had stuffed it in his back pocket and never mentioned anything about it.

"No, Vike said to keep details to us, so we have time to use it to our advantage. We don't want the law hot on our heels if we're hunting."

"Understandable."

Torch speaks up. "You need to bring some shit here, so you can stay with her."

"I figured that. I already told her I wasn't going to leave."

His brow hikes. "Oh yeah? I didn't see her throw any blows."

"I know, I think she's still in shock, so it didn't even register all the way. I was expecting her to fight me tooth and nail. I'm sure she'll let me have it when this place clears out."

"One of us can come switch with you tomorrow for a few hours so you can get some of your shit."

"Appreciate it. You think this has to do with the biker that was hanging around here yesterday that she called us about?"

Odin agrees. "Hell yes. I'd bet money on it too. They clearly have Chevelle in their sights. It sucks for her. If we weren't here, she'd most likely end up dead or kidnapped. Luckily, we caught it before things escalated to that."

I draw in a quick breath, picturing those stupid fucks taking her and knowing just a few of the things they'd do to her. "I can't let her get hurt."

"We agree with you. Trust me, this is Viking and Ares' prayers getting answered. They've been sitting on the sidelines waiting to find these guys and have a reason to take them out. They've fucked with our club enough. Now it's just about finding their locations. Each one of these fucks that comes around, we snatch them and question as much as possible."

"Good. I'll keep my eyes peeled."

"You'll need to, they tend to be sneaky," Odin supplies.

"Then we should set up a trap." A menacing grin overtakes my lips as I begin to think of what I need to make sure we have our chance to extract information out of every Fist that comes snooping around. "I need horse tranquilizer," I say seriously, and Odin smiles.

"This is going to be fun."

"I'm going to use them as target practice from four floors up. Make sure you have a truck at the ready."

"You got it," he agrees, and I fist bump them both.

8. **She was just another broken doll,**

dreaming of a boy with glue.

- Atticus

MERCENARY

"I agreed to you sticking around here. I never said you could stay in my apartment." Chevelle continues to argue with me. Ever since I followed her to her apartment, she's been giving me hell.

"You keep talking as if I'm asking you. I'm not asking shit, woman. I need this window, and it happens to be in your apartment."

"It's my bedroom window, where I sleep!"

"I can take a break from hunting these assholes to fuck you if that's what you're asking for. Seems like you may need a good hard fuck to get you to chill the fuck out."

"Jesus, you're hardheaded."

"I was just thinking the exact same thing about you."

"Fine, I'll sleep on the couch."

I glance around, noticing she doesn't even have a couch. There's a bathroom and a small kitchen area. The only real furniture she has here is a big chair and her bed. "Scared?"

"Excuse me?" she hisses, her tone turning deadly. She can't handle being challenged; she likes to win far too much. It makes her a badass, but it's also a weakness if she doesn't know when to back down.

"I asked if you were scared. You're acting like a chickenshit over sleeping in the same room as a man."

"Oh, that's rich. You know damn well I can kick your ass if need be. I'm *not* scared of you."

I snort but keep quiet. It's enough of a response to make her cheeks flush. Fucking shit it makes her even sexier watching her get all wound up. Is this how she'd look riding my cock? I don't have to worry about falling asleep tonight if she does actually sleep in here. My stiff dick is way too uncomfortable to get any rest around her.

I lay my arm across my lap and glance out to the parking lot. Her mouthy replies and tight figure are too much to take. I want to toss her across the bed, pin her with my body and make her give in to all of my desires. She could just lay there naked and let me stare at her all night. I can wait to fuck her if she lets me drink in her curves and pink folds for hours on end.

I need to fuck someone before this gets out of control. Sure, I've chased pussy, but they've always given in nearly right away. Chevelle though, she's a tough bitch, acting like I don't affect her in any way. I know her pussy's wet though. she can pretend all she wants that she doesn't eat up the attention I give her, but I can smell her sex. Mix it in with her resolve, and she's like the forbidden fruit just taunting me to take a bite. I'd bite in a fucking heartbeat too. She just needs to bend a little more and admit that she wants me to fuck her.

"And what was that shit down there? I should've spoken to the cops, this is my business." She glares at me, scrambling for something to fight with me about to change the subject away from my previous challenge.

My brow raises, ready to put this woman across my knee. "You can't say thank you, can you?"

"You expect me to thank you? For what? Having me sit back like some meek little woman? I don't think so, biker boy."

"You need your ass spanked," I growl, and she shoots off the bed.

"Try it," she hisses, coming to stand in front of me. She's way too close for us to be arguing like this. With the amount of untapped sexual tension between us, I may snap.

I get to my feet, leaning away from the wall I was propped against and tower over her smaller frame. I made the mistake of underestimating her the first time. I'll never do that again. Being slammed on my back once was too many times for me. "Be careful what you wish for, you might just get it."

Her eyes flare. "You're not man enough," she breathes.

It was the wrong thing to say. I'd have kept going back and forth with her all night if she'd persisted, but that comment, nope. She's used to weak men; I'm not one of them. My hand flies to her throat, grip tight enough to hold her in place and my arm span keeps her far enough away to retaliate.

"You've mistaken," I growl. "You caught me off guard before, but sweetie, you've met your match." At that, I hook a leg behind hers, twisting her in the process, so we hit the floor with me over her back. I do my best to not squish her beneath me, but she's got too many moves that I have to focus on subduing her more. My other hand takes over, clamping the back of her neck and I release the front, keeping her face to the ground.

I reach back and smack her ass through her jeans and lean forward, breathing against her throat. "Want another?"

"I hate you!" she screams furiously. She's so pissed it's hard for me to hold back my pleased chuckle.

I smack her ass again, and she makes a feline growl sound that I find deliciously toxic. It's her being completely livid, but it turns me on further.

Leaning back down, I rub my nose behind her ear, taking in her scent. She smells like sugary vanilla. I wonder if she tastes like it too. "Another?"

"Fuck you," she hisses, and I chuckle.

My warm breath flutters over her flesh. "I wish," I admit with a grumble and draw her lobe between my teeth. "But not tonight, I have to work." I finish and sit up then spank her again.

She does this angry scream thing in the back of her throat. I'm pretty sure if I let her up now she'll attempt to kill me.

"Be a good girl, or I'll keep going."

"You better pray you never sleep!"

My palm rests on her ass, and I laugh again. "I could sleep with you under me...naked." My hand spans enough to barely caress her between her thighs. Her folds are probably swollen and red, begging to be fucked. God how I'd love to see them right now and lick her clean.

"Let me up."

I spank her ass again, and her breathing becomes labored, morphing into more of a pant. She's turned on—she likes it as much as I do.

"Say please."

"Please, fuck off."

"You won't get rid of me that easily. Now, you gonna play nice, or should I keep spanking you?"

"I don't play nice," she admits and wiggles her hips.

"I know; that's why I can't get enough of you. Tell me Chevelle, are you wet right now?"

"Shut up."

My palm smacks down as I deliver another spanking, "You were doing well for a minute."

She takes a deep breath, exhaling, and she mumbles, "Will you please get off of me?"

Bending back over, my tongue trails along her lobe, my excited breath warming her ear as I demand, "Tell me if you're wet."

I wait with bated breath, not expecting her to answer honestly. I'm surprised she hasn't bucked me off by now.

"Soaked."

"Your panties or pussy?"

"Both."

"You've made me a happy man," I confess, rubbing my nose against her gently one last time before climbing to my feet. I head straight to the bathroom to take care of my hard on. My dick's so stiff right now if I don't get some type of relief I'll puke later from the serious case of blue balls. I've never needed to feel a woman wrapped around my shaft so badly before in my life.

CHEVELLE

He storms to the bathroom, and I couldn't be more thankful for the small reprieve. My cheeks are flushed and burning from admitting the truth to him. I'm mortified over what just happened — that I let him gain the upper hand — and the fact that I enjoyed every second of it.

He's infuriating, always arguing with everything I have to say and being so damn good-looking while doing it. I was ready to hand him an ass kicking, and then his hand just shot out of nowhere catching me by surprise. I'm going to have to store that move. Not that I'm big enough to use it myself, but I'll be damned if another man gets the jump on me like that again.

Climbing to my feet, I step to the window he was busily peering out of before I tried to pick a fight with him. I'm not used to having anyone in this space, especially at nighttime. If I want to sleep with a man, I go elsewhere — never in my home.

Mercenary just strolls in and takes over everything like he owns the place. How can he be so blasé about sticking around here so much? People have come and gone throughout my life. I learned at a young age to not expect them to stick around and having him here like this feels as if it's crossing a barrier or something. I know it's for my protection, even if I don't want to admit out loud that I need it. It's all nerve-wracking. I'm used to taking care of myself.

I blink and register the figure across the street propped up against the light post. Shit. I wonder if Mercenary saw him too.

With a few quick hops, I bang on the bathroom door and receive a grunt in response.

"Cupcake?"

"In a minute," he grumbles.

"There's someone outside."

"Fuck!" He swears and follows it up with a groan. I hear the sink turn on and jump back. I don't want him to think I was standing here listening to him do whatever he was doing. Although I have a good guess he was in there stroking his cock. I wonder if he's hung long and hard or if he's more blunt and wide?

Damn it. He has my mind constantly in the freaking gutter around him. He's pure sex on two legs, and I can't seem to help myself when I'm in his presence. It's already bad enough I needed to put on a new pair of underwear and got zero relief from him taunting my pussy earlier.

The door opens, and he steps through, cheeks still pink with his breaths coming heavy.

"Have a good time?" I ask with an amused grin. I'm such a bitch sometimes, I laugh to myself.

"Would've been better if it was your mouth," he responds gruffly and strides to the window. "Where did you see them?"

"Him. I saw one man. He's across the street, by the light post."

His head tilts for a brief second before straightening and reaching for the CO2 fed gun. "Son of a bitch. I think he's too far away."

"I could create a distraction, maybe get him to come closer?"

"How do you figure?"

"I can go outside; maybe he'll cross the street."

He snorts and mimics my voice, not sounding even remotely close. "And maybe he'll put a bullet in you the first chance he gets."

"Okay smartass. I just figured he'd want my money, not my life."

"Because the bomb earlier didn't clue you in enough?"

"You're a dick, you know that?"

"Maybe if I had some relief I wouldn't be so dickish."

"Dickish? Did you just make that up?"

He shrugs.

"You're just pissed because he's too far away. It's not my fault you don't know how to shoot."

With a growl, his glare lands on me. "Woman…"

The word's enough of a threat to shut me up. Clearly, he doesn't find me distracting him right now very amusing. Instead of arguing further, I whisper, "I'm making some tea then." Not sure why I whisper since we're inside this giant building and the guy's across the street, but I do.

He nods, silent and I tiptoe toward my shoebox sized kitchen. I need to do something to get my mind distracted and making tea seems to be the easiest option to put a little distance between us. I don't know how I plan on getting any sleep with him here like this. My place is a studio, which means the only real room that has any privacy is the bathroom. Even now when I'm busily digging through my cabinet to hunt down lemon and chamomile tea bags, I can easily watch him from across the room.

I find the gray box and pull two bags free and heat the water. Once it's hot enough, I pour two cups with a tea bag in each, grab some spoons and a bottle of honey. With light feet, I make my way until I'm beside him and can set the cups on the small table off to the side of us.

"Did he move?" I whisper and peer through the pane of glass.

"Nah." He swallows, and my gaze lands on the same man as before. He's still there in the same position.

I peer up at Mercenary, taking in his relaxed stance. You'd think he'd be uptight since he's planning on shooting the guy, even if it is with a tranquilizer. He's not though. You'd think it was just another day on the job for him. Maybe it is. "Is this sorta thing normal for you?"

With a huff, he flicks his gaze to mine. "Do you need attention or something? I already spanked your ass once tonight."

With a glower, I spin around and busy myself by removing my tea bag and stirring in some honey. I was going to be nice, but he can take his tea bitter. I smirk to myself and bring my cup along with the bottle of honey with me to sit in my favorite overstuffed chair.

9. **Girls that like fast cars and racing aren't weird, they're a rare gift from God.**

- Carmemes.com

MERCENARY

"Where's Chevelle?" Odin asks as he and Nightmare help me load the comatose Iron Fist into the back of the pickup truck.

"She fell asleep watching me wait to shoot this asshole."

He chuckles. "Guess you can go have some fun with her now."

"I wish. The bitch is dead set on me living my life with blue balls. I didn't even enjoy tranqing this guy, my dick hurt too badly."

They both laugh. *Fuckers.*

"It's true. I had to spank her ass earlier to get her to simmer down. Probably would've lost my shit if she hadn't fallen asleep eventually."

"She never would've gone for that," he argues and Night nods his agreement.

"I didn't give her a choice, brother. I spanked her several times." With a shrug, I grumble. "She'll learn I won't allow her to push me around."

"Jesus, brother." Nightmare shakes his head. "Be careful. Before you know it, you'll be putting your name on her back."

"I'm not looking to add a property patch to her, although can't say I'd mind too much if it ended in that."

"Damn," Odin grins. "It's only been a week Merc."

A sigh leaves me, thinking how tight she's already wound me up. "You think I don't know that? Shit, Saint and Sinner must be thrilled. At this rate, I have no time to fuck with Jude. And someone's going to win that damn bet."

'That's a positive on your part," he says and Night grunts in agreement. "Having a thing for their woman would've ended in them killing you."

"We'll have to agree to disagree."

Nightmare snorts. "Give it time, you just got here. Wait until you see them play with their food. My name may be Nightmare, but they're the shit nightmares are made of."

I've yet to see this craziness that multiple brothers have warned me of, and part of me wonders if it's mostly just hype. Viking's the brother that strikes me as the one not to cross out of all of them. Any man who carries around an axe like it's an everyday utensil should be taken into consideration. Just like Torch—the brother fucking torches people. I wouldn't fuck with him, that's for sure.

He slams the tailgate shut, and I step back. "You want me to keep shooting them and calling you if any others show up?"

O nods. "Yeah as long as it's just onesies and twosies. Any more than that call for reinforcements 'cause it'll mean they want to do more than just keep an eye on The Pit."

"All right, brother," I agree, and fist bump them before pulling the metal bay door down and locking it. I hope no others decide to show up tonight, but so far, they've been fairly resilient. I'd like to get some kind of sleep tonight, especially if Chevelle plans to keep me on my toes.

Arriving back to her place, I find her still curled up in the chair fast asleep. She's so sweet and innocent looking when she's like this. It's when she's awake that her mouth has a sharp sting to it.

I scoop her into my arms, her body tilting and curling into me like a sleepy cat. I could get used to having her in my arms, all pliant and safe but I won't hold my breath on it happening. Pushing the covers away, I lay her down, tugging her free of her tight jeans. She stirs but lets me remove them, leaving her in her tank and panties. I snuggle her under the fluffy blanket before crawling into the spot beside her.

I'm on my back, staring at the ceiling when she shifts toward me. Her arm goes around my waist, her nose tucking into my bicep. She's fucking adorable, a goddamn wildcat and having her close to naked has me wanting her fiercely. She's asleep, and it's probably the only chance I'll get to really stare my fill.

I watch her for a moment before leaning over and pressing a kiss to her temple. She doesn't say anything, but I feel her hand pull me to her, tightening around my hip a bit more and I can't help but wonder if she's faking sleep. That's fine if she is, if she feels the need to pretend to be asleep in order to touch me, I'll roll with it. After all, it's just one more step in the direction I want her to go.

I wake to an empty bed and glance around to discover I'm alone in the apartment as well. What did I expect? Waking up to breakfast in bed or some shit? Chevelle made it clear she doesn't cook, so my mind shouldn't even be going there. Shit, I should've woken up early and done that for her. It would've caught her off guard even more. Stubborn female.

With a stretch and a massive yawn, I head for the window to see if dumbass has been replaced.

"Motherfucker," I grumble and grab my burner from the jeans pocket on the floor.

"Odin," the VP answers.

"You won't fucking believe this."

"What?"

"There's someone hanging from the pole out front."

"Wait, what?"

"That damn light pole...it looks like a giant bolt has been screwed into it. There's a body hanging from it, rope around their neck. From here it definitely looks like they're dead."

"Fuck, fuck, fuck! Viking is going to be pissed. I'll send Torch and Nightmare to go collect the body."

"Did you get anything out of the guy from last night?"

"He hasn't woken up yet, those horse tranquilizers are strong."

"Apparently. He's not dead, right?"

"Not yet, anyhow."

I grunt. "You want me to go out there and get the body down?"

"No, stay inside with Chevelle, just in case they're waiting for you to leave her vulnerable."

"Shit, I haven't even seen her yet. I just woke up."

"Go find her and make sure she's okay."

"I will."

"Later."

"Later," I reply and end the call then yank on my pants and boots and head out of the studio.

CHEVELLE

"You weren't there when I woke up." Mercenary comes up on the other side of the hood. I was just checking the plugs before clocking my time.

"I thought you'd be tired from being up all night." I tiptoed around, not wanting to wake him. He looked dead to the world with how hard he was sleeping.

"I was. What are you doing?" His cool blue irises run over me like he's famished and I'm breakfast.

"Checking plugs then I planned to run this pretty lady to get my latest track time. I put new tires on her a week ago, and I'm not quite used to them."

He nods. "You probably shouldn't drive right now."

My back stiffens as I stand to my full height and sputter, "Excuse me?" The man has a lot of nerve; I have no doubt about that.

"A bomb went off yesterday," he emphasis slowly, tilting his head like I'm nuts. "It's smart to not drive your cars right now."

"But it's what I do," I argue. He's lost his mind telling me not to drive. It's like having your favorite toy and not being able to touch it. That doesn't sit well for me. I learned at a young age that if I want something to go for it, to take it. Waiting around gets you nowhere and nothing to show for it.

"You'll be safer if you take a short break, just a week or two."

"Yeah, that's not happening." Not to mention that's asking me to take a ten thousand dollar cut to my monthly pay. It definitely won't be going down while I have anything to say about it.

He throws his hands up dramatically, and I hold back my smirk. "Fuck, woman, why do you have to be so damn difficult?"

I stomp around the front of the car coming face to face with the grouchy male who's decided to rudely interrupt my quiet morning time. "Listen here, cupcake, go eat a fucking banana or whatever it is you need to take it down a notch. Racing is my job, it's my life. I won't stop just because it gets a little dangerous. Racing is not safe, that's partly why it's so damn fun."

"I know," he admits, catching me off guard.

"You know?"

He nods. "I get it. I wouldn't stop if someone told me to either. At least let me check your car over before you go cranking the engine and taking off."

I release a breath through my clenched teeth, unaware I was even holding it. He wants to check my car over to see if it has a bomb in it. That's pretty freaking sweet. Why can't he always be like this? "Yeah, sure, I can deal with that. Thanks."

He tilts his head toward me slightly and then crouches to slide under the car. On the way down he gripes, "By the way, it's eat a Snickers bar, not a banana."

"Ugh, did you just correct me?"

"Well, the commercial isn't about bananas." He calls from the ground.

"Un-freaking-believable! You just can't help yourself from correcting me and being in control, can you?"

He rolls out, opening the trunk to snoop around there next. "Oh, I'm the difficult one?"

"Yes, you are. I do not remember this much stress in my life before you showed up."

He pokes his head out, meeting my stare. "All this over a banana?"

"Holy shit," I hiss and stomp away.

I go straight to one of the concession stands. They're all locked up, but the benefits of owning the place is I have a key to everything. I grab a king-sized Snickers bar and also a banana from the walk-in cooler. I knew we'd have them because one thing we offer is banana splits with hand scooped ice cream. Surprisingly they're one of the concessions top sellers.

I'm still stomping around when I make my way back down the stairs to the center and find Mercenary leaning up against my car. He's propped against the shiny paint all nonchalant, arms crossed over his chest, muscles bulging while wearing a cocky smirk. He looks every ounce of a badass, and so help me God, do I want to jump his bones.

"All done. Your car's safe for you to drive in circles now." He winks, and I toss the candy and fruit in his direction. Surprisingly he has reflexes like a cat and snatches them in midair.

"Two hands?" I gape.

"I'm ambidextrous," he shrugs and opens his fingers to see what I threw.

"You went to get me one of each?" His wide eyes meet mine.

I nod, biting the inside of my cheek.

He drops them to the ground and with a few powerful strides, stops in front of me. I'm about to rip into him for being ungrateful when his hands cup my cheeks and his lips meet mine. My world seems to stop as his mouth roots me in place. My mind and body fight each other, one tells me to fuck him while the other screams for me to thrash against him. What is it with this man that has me teetering on the edge of control?

He coaxes my mouth open, parting my lips to dip inside with his tongue. It twists with mine, caressing me, forcing my resolve to weaken. We fight each other for control, teeth clashing, and tongues sparring to gain control. I feel like I'm falling, but it's only Mercenary pushing me to the ground. His heat encompasses around me, warming like an electric blanket. His knee parts my thighs, wedging his way where I've craved him to be since I first laid eyes on him.

Rocking my hips, I flip him to the side, climbing over to straddle his groin without breaking our kiss. His hands land on my upper thighs, pulling me to him and grinding into my core. Groans escape from both of us at the delicious friction, and our kiss takes a turn to become more dirty than angry.

The craving to have this man underneath me, naked, while I bounce on his cock has my skin breaking out in cold chills like an icy wind just came out of nowhere. My nipples grow hard under my tank top, and a whimper breaks free as our tongues tangle with each other. I want to tie him up and fuck him until his dick no longer stands up.

"Uh, Chevy?" Ace's curious voice in the distance breaks through my Mercenary induced foggy brain.

He continues yammering on. "Sorry to uh, bother you guys, but the truck's here and the driver needs you to sign before he can start unloading."

"Shit," leaves me in a breathy huff as I pull back. My lustful gaze locking on Mercenary's lowered lashes as he stares back, lazily, irises portraying he wants to fuck me just as badly.

"I love Snickers," he rumbles after a second of our trance, and I smirk.

"Good, cupcake, eat up." With that, I stand and follow Ace toward the loading bay.

10. **If anyone can have it,**

I don't want it...

- Smart women

MERCENARY

I'm eating the banana Chevelle gave me when my brothers stroll into The Pit, finding me on my ass, stuffing my face. Odin's blond brow hikes, his stony expression reminding me of his older brother, Viking. "We interrupting your breakfast?"

Swallowing, I shake my head. "I have a feeling this is going to be breakfast and lunch. You guys get the body?"

"Yeah, I can't believe the stupid fuckers strung him up out in the open," Torch gripes and Nightmare grunts in agreement.

"Me either. Is it just you guys or did the other brothers ride over with you?"

Nightmare tucks his dark, shoulder-length hair behind his ears. "Just us. The rest were too hung over."

I nod. The lucky asses getting to drink and relax last night. I was here keeping watch for Iron Fists to pop up all night. My eyes feel like they've been pricked by needles from the little sleep I was able to get.

"They got the Fist to talk; we found one of their locations too."

"No shit?" I ask O, and he confirms. No wonder they were celebrating. I've heard a few times how they've been waiting for years to lock down this rival club.

"Vike doesn't believe it all, of course. He thinks there's another spot they're either hiding, maybe more or something else we don't know about."

"Possibly three spots? You think they'd be that organized to have the club spread out in three locations?"

"Probably," Torch says and leans against Chevelle's Nova.

"Careful brother, if the bitch sees you on her car she'll flip."

He snorts. "I'm not so easily intimidated."

Odin scoffs. "If you had any sense of self-preservation you would be when it comes to her."

Rather than argue, I open the Snickers and take a big bite. She even got me the king-sized bar. It's the best one. I get done chewing and ask, "What'd you do with the body?"

Nightmare grins. "It's rolled in a tarp and loaded in the truck. I'm gonna let Saint feed it to the pigs at the farm. Looks like it was one of their prospects. I think they got nervous that someone ratted them out or whatever, so they killed one of their own."

A shiver overcomes me imagining the hogs eating the body. I'm a hardened biker, but that shit's gross—even for me. "You guys had good timing. The delivery truck showed up, must have been right after you got the body down or I'm sure we'd be hearing sirens about now."

"The last thing we need is the cops catching wind of this," Odin gripes and we all nod, agreeing. None of us want to end up in jail, especially for crimes we didn't commit. "Prez wants you at the club for church tomorrow. He said to bring Chevelle with you, so she's not left here alone."

"Bet, text me the time, and we'll be there."

"Yeah, good luck with getting her to go with you."

"I'll probably talk her into going for food and then just stop at the club. She won't have a choice."

Odin snorts. "You think she'll actually let you drive? Keep dreaming, brother."

"I'm going to stick her on my bike. She won't have a say in the matter."

"How you going to manage that?"

"It'll be her idea." I grin, and they chuckle.

"You ever been on a motorcycle before mine?" I ask as she bites into her taco.

She chews a few times and then replies. "A Ducati but not a bike like yours, no."

Who the fuck had a Ducati for her to ride? My Harley is nice, but probably not as smooth of a ride as an expensive ass Ducati. Wonder who the lucky prick was that had her and was too stupid not to hold on to her? What a dumbass. I never would've let her go had it been me. Rather than demand a name and social security number to hunt him down, I take a swig from my beer and move on.

"What did you think of the ride?"

"Surprisingly, I enjoyed it. I can see why you guys like it so much, kind of reminds me of when I race."

"That's because I was hauling ass with you, figured you'd appreciate the speed and adrenaline."

She nods and licks her lips. She misses some salsa just under her bottom lip, and I reach forward. Swiping my finger to catch the salsa, I bring it to my mouth and her eyes flair.

"Salsa," I rasp.

She grabs the finger I just had between my lips and brings it to her mouth, sucking it. Her tongue swipes the tip, and the stroke instantly has my imagination running wild, wanting my cock to be in its place. A growl escapes as my groin tightens, wanting to yank her across the table at the fucking taco shack. She's lucky she's not mine, or I'd take her out back and have her sucking my cock off and fucking her across my bike in a heartbeat.

"Maybe I didn't want to share," she taunts after releasing my hand.

"We need to go." I manage to choke out, staring her down.

"But I'm not done."

"I have church to get to and any more time watching that mouth, I'm gonna be fucking it."

Her cheeks heat as her breaths increase in speed. Her chest moves with her heavy breathing and her lids lower, irises dilating at my proclamation. She wants me to fuck her. She wants me to take her decision away so when she fights me on it, she can pretend she doesn't want it as badly as I do.

"You're pretty damn bossy, biker."

"And you're sexy as fuck. You want to suck my cock or head to the clubhouse? This is the only time I'm going to ask before I make the decision for you." It's enough of a threat to piss her off. She doesn't like to be bossed, and I love having control. We're like fire and fire, both burning hot and demanding, both vying for full control.

She stands with a huff. "I'll get a to go bag." She stomps off to the counter, and I watch her swing her plump ass with each step. The young cabana looking guy smiles, and turns on the charm, thinking he can flirt with her, probably planning to ask for her number. I should knock his damn teeth out looking at my woman like that.

Gritting my teeth, I chug the remaining beer to cool off my temper. I don't need to get arrested at the damn taco joint for a kid merely getting through puberty. I'd really appear like a damn jackoff to Chevelle then. Witnessing her smile for him has me wanting to lock her in my room back at the compound. None of my brothers would give two shits if I kept her as mine. Fuck, she'd be pissed if I did. She'd probably slit my throat the first chance she got. *Stubborn female.*

"A little friendly, huh? You like 'em young?" I grumble once she comes back and begins loading the rest of our food into a paper bag to take with us. I ordered like twenty tacos, so I'd have some for dinner too. Chevelle wasn't screwing around when she said she doesn't cook.

She glowers my way. "I like them when they aren't assholes, not that it's any of your business."

"Too bad." I get to my feet and don't tip, cause fuck that guy getting my money.

"Hmm?" Chevelle hums with a frown. She's a badass, but she's way too curious. It's her downfall and has been the way to get her to let her wall down with me.

"'Cause I'm an asshole," I shrug and strut toward the door, shooting a glare at the guy behind the counter. He stares at Chevy for a moment, but it's quickly broken when he catches my look. His eyes suddenly find the counter in front of him pretty damn interesting. Smart move on his part. I don't start a lot of shit, but I do tend to be territorial when it comes to a woman I'm interested in.

She follows me to my bike. "Why were you looking at him like that?" she asks, catching up to me.

"He was interested in you."

"So? I'm here like three times a week, sometimes four. He's used to me."

"No," I hiss. "He *likes* you."

She shrugs, and I snatch the bag, securing it in my saddlebag and throw my leg over to take my seat. "It's not really a big deal." She places her palm on my shoulder and climbs on behind me. She adjusts until she's snug up to my back.

"The hell it isn't. The kid won't be able to speak if I catch him looking at you like that again." I promise and start my engine, drowning out any argument she may have. I'm being obnoxious, but after the kiss we shared, she's overtaken that possessiveness I have inside. She hasn't smiled at me like that yet, and I have a feeling that's what pisses me off the most out of the entire situation.

"Just take me back."

"I wanted you at the club with me."

"I'll go another time. I have an order coming in."

"You just had one."

"I get deliveries nearly every day. I don't want to argue about it."

"But you'll be alone."

"I'm a grown-ass woman, and I'm not alone. I have employees there."

"I don't like it."

"You can drop me off, or I can walk."

I crank the engine and take off. She jerks to hold on to me tightly, and I smirk. She deserved that jolt, arguing with me over this shit. I drop her off without exchanging a single word. Leaving her there has a bad taste in my mouth growing stronger and stronger. It's pointless to try and talk her out of it though; she's the type that really would walk back, cursing me the entire time.

The ride passes quickly, with the air hot and dry. It's another summer day in Texas, and my body hasn't adjusted to the temperature change yet. In Chicago, we'd all bitch it was too warm, but I had no idea what real heat was until coming here. The weather may say ninety-five degrees, but it has a goddamn heat index of a hundred and ten. That shit just makes me want to stay inside, kind of like Chicago winters.

I'm the last one to sit down, and it's not my favorite thing in the world to have everyone's attention on me all at once.

11. **Here's to strong women.**

May we know them.

May we be them.

May we raise them.

MERCENARY

"Nice of you to join us," Prez grumbles as I get comfortable and set my beer down on the large table. "In session," he states and slams the gavel down. The wood landing on the table is loud enough that the sound bounces off the walls and I have to hold myself still not to cringe. The brothers would give me a ton of shit if they witnessed me jump from the damn gavel.

"The three Fists we brought in have been talking. Leisurely, unfortunately, but at least we're getting some kind of information from them. We have two confirmed locations for their compounds so far, and until we get any others out of them, Ruger is actively searching between the areas."

Viking's cousin, Blaze, speaks up. "So you believe they'll all be close together."

He nods. "Yeah, it makes sense. It'd be easy enough for them to get to each other but safer to be spread out."

Prez has a point. The other Oath Keepers charter is about twenty minutes away from here; it's convenient for the brothers to go back and forth. It's also just far enough away from each other to deter a rival club trying to take us all out at once. The Iron Fists tried at one time but most of the club was gone and missed the hit, so in the end, the Fists failed.

"Once we find the locations and know for sure there are no others close enough to dole out immediate retaliation on us, we'll hit. We have to be certain though. This is us calling for war once we hit them, and I, for one, have breathed a bit easier having this supposed truce."

Nightmare's fist slams on the table. "Fuck the truce. I want their lives. Puppet's death is mine for the taking, and I want to see the motherfucker filleted and burned to ash for touching my family."

Viking winces at the outburst and agrees. "Yes brother, I gave you my word you'd have your revenge. When it's time, we'll coordinate with Ares' club."

"How will we get close enough to them?" Odin asks.

"Ares will split up his brothers and set one of the Fists' compounds on fire then hold back to catch any remaining stragglers that may make it out alive. We'll take whatever necessary precautions and storm the main clubhouse. Unless we can get ahold of Puppet, the Iron Fists' head president, another way. If that happens, then we just sit back and blow the third clubhouse sky high somehow."

Torch grunts. "And the cops?" He's always the one thinking about repercussions from the law.

"The sheriff will look the other way if it's in his jurisdiction. He wants the Fists gone. They've caused too many problems, and he's been friends with my ol' lady's pops for far too long. His loyalty lies with the club if it gets rid of one of his problems."

Torch shakes his head. "You can never trust the cops."

Prez sighs. "Relax, T, I've taken care of it." He turns to the brothers across from me. "Saint and Sinner, I want you both to ride up to meet with Ruger. He's caught wind of someone following him, and he may need some backup."

"Bet," Sinner agrees.

"About time we get to have some fun," Saint grins manically.

Prez turns to Smokey. "Make sure to send them with some extra cash for the hotels and shit. Keep me posted on the books."

Smokey nods, taking a drag of his cigarette.

"Odin and Torch, you both need to hit The Pit tonight." They agree, and he continues. "Anything else?"

We stay quiet.

"Do your fucking job and get the hell out of here. Church is over." He slams the gavel down, and we all rise. "Mercenary." The Prez calls my name before I take a step.

"Yeah?"

"Hold back a sec; I need to have a chat with you."

This can't be good. We're bikers, we don't 'chat.' "What's up?" I sit back in my spot at the other end of the table. I'm the newest here, so I sit the farthest away from him.

"You need to sit tight tonight."

"Excuse me? I have a race." I'm not staying at the club; I have to protect Chevelle.

He shakes his head. "I'm sending Torch in your place."

My throat nearly closes up thinking of him with Chevelle. I choke out, "Excuse me?"

With a shrug, he lets out a sigh. "I spoke to Chevelle earlier."

"And?" When was this? It had to be when I dropped her off. That was the only time she was out of my sight besides when she showered.

"Well, she wants you out of The Pit tonight."

"You have to be fucking kidding me."

"I'm not."

"Did she say why?"

"You told her you didn't want her to race?"

I nod. "Of course, I did, it's too dangerous. She could be in the next car that explodes."

"Can't do that brother." He chuckles and takes a sip from the tumbler in front of him.

"The hell I can't." He may be the President of this club, but he's no one to tell me who I can and cannot fuck. I'll decide that on my own.

He waits for a few beats, thinking over what he wants to say before speaking again. "You don't tame a wild bitch by holding her down. You set her free and give her strength. You try to snuff out her passion for living, and she'll never stick around. You take control and show her you have her back and she flourishes, standing beside you."

That's probably the most poetic shit I've ever heard come from the Prez's mouth. "I won't let her kill herself because of stupid arrogance. The woman is bullheaded and is going to be the death of both of us."

"She probably thinks you're acting the same way."

Huffing, I get to my feet.

"I mean it, Mercenary. Torch goes in your place tonight." He points, and I bristle.

"No disrespect Prez, but this is between her and me, not Torch. I can't believe she called you. I'd just had my damn tongue in her mouth yesterday."

"You're wrong. This is about my club dealing with their enemy. You have one thing on your mind, which is fine, but you need to take your blinders off. This is bigger than your cock wanting some forbidden pussy."

"I've gotten you the Fists to question so far, not anyone else."

"And I'm grateful for it, but what happens if ten of them showed up? Could you make the right moves and think long enough to call in your brothers and also protect yourself? They could fuck you up and demand information out of you. Can you honestly say you can do what is needed or will she have you so distracted you risk your neck for her first?"

Fuck. He has a point.

"So, have Torch and Odin in the stands again like last week. I'll be down on the track to protect Chevelle. Then it all works out, and everyone's straight."

"She doesn't want you there at all. You'll step in and attempt to stop her from racing and you can't. That's her damn track; she's the one letting us be there in the first place."

"I'm not one to usually go against orders, but I'm at least having a conversation with her ass about this. I won't let her hide behind a phone because I'm not there in person to talk some sense into her stubborn head."

"Don't fuck this up, Mercenary. We need to have a spot there to get our info, and if you screw with that, you'll have me on your ass."

"Noted," I mutter with a huff and head for the door. My muscles are coiled extra tight with irritation. I have to see Chevelle; she needs to realize she can't call the Prez every time we disagree on something. I can't believe she took it that far rather than fighting with me about it. She must've realized I was serious when I told her I didn't want her in those damn cars tonight.

I pay no attention to any of my brothers as I storm through the bar for my motorcycle. The machine can't carry me fast enough it seems, and my anger only grows with the longer it takes me to reach her. The woman fights me at every turn, and now she believes she can get her way by going through my Prez.

I've never met a female who didn't give into me by now. Normally I'd have fucked them, and they'd be doing whatever I asked until I got tired of them. I've barely kissed this bitch, and she's put me on my ass. It's gotten to the point where I even spanked her, and she didn't fully submit. She's going to be the death of me one way or another.

I shake my head, pushing my bike's speed up higher. The scenery off on each side of the road passes in a blur. I don't pay any attention to it anyhow. I'm too distracted, thinking of only Chevelle and how I can get her to finally listen. The Pit comes up on my left, and I lower my speed, pulling into the parking lot and going around to the backside.

I'm met at the large silver bay door as I roll it up. My gaze instantly falls to the man lying at Chevelle's feet, draining any irritation I was harboring on the ride over. "Where'd he come from?" I nod to the unconscious man on the floor.

His leather cut gives him away as being another Iron Fist. Odin was right; they're like damn cockroaches never going away. It makes me wonder just how large their club really is. Odin said most likely fifty to a hundred members, and that's just in this general area. That's a lot of damn bikers for any club.

She shrugs, tucking her dark hair behind her ears all innocent like. "When you left they just showed up."

"They?"

"There's another knocked out over by the front. He was too fat for me to drag him to this door."

"Damn it." I flick my eyes over her. "You fight them? They hurt you?"

"No." She shakes her head, and I let out a relived breath. I'm very aware that she's tough, but they could've ended up hurting her. Thinking of these fuck faces showing up to do who knows what to her, has my chest swelling, wanting to dole out punishing blows to keep her safe. "I shot them with the tranq darts. I was looking out the window in my place when I first noticed them walking toward the front."

A wide grin grows on my face, despite the danger. "You shot them both?" I didn't know she could shoot. Jesus, can this woman not do anything? If my cock wasn't so enormous, she'd have me questioning my manhood. She makes everything seem easy. It's hard being so tempted by a woman who knows how to do everything you do and do some of it even better than you can.

She nods, a sheepish smile taking over. "You had that damn gun, and I wanted to shoot it. They finally gave me a good enough reason to use it without ruffling your feathers."

A loud laugh escapes me, and I pull her to me. "You know somethin'?"

"Hmm?" She hikes an eyebrow up and tilts her head to meet my eyes.

"You're a bad bitch, Chevy. I've never met another like you," I admit and a blush steals over her cheeks.

She lets the nickname slide with my compliment. "I hope that's a good thing?" she whispers, and I lean in, so my lips nearly touch hers.

"It's a damn good thing, sweetie." With my hands on her shoulders, I pull her the last step to me and plant my mouth on hers. She meets me with so much fervor in return that my body screams for more. I walk her backward to the wall, my hands reaching down and sliding up the backs of her thighs, never breaking our kiss.

My palms lift her, spreading her legs and her arms clutch onto my neck as I rest my cock against her center. Holding her up against the cement wall, I kiss her roughly. My body's beyond turned on, knowing she knocked these guys out and drug them inside and she didn't even freak out about it at all. Chevelle really is a badass, and that's so damn sexy.

Grinding into her core, my palms slide from under her ass up along her thighs and under her tank top. They glide along her ribs, my thumbs only pausing when they can rub across her breasts and play with her nipples. My fingers move back and forth, caressing and squeezing her breasts until she moans in pleasure and arches her back, pushing into my hands even more.

"I want you. I need in this pussy," I confess with a gruff voice, thick with desire. My heavy cock pushes against her, grinding in circles. I love having her like this, panting and needy. She wants me as badly as I want her. I have to make her give in to me.

With another groan into my mouth, her hands push my chest with enough force, I break away, blinking a few times to clear my lustful haze she's drowning me in. "What is it, Chevelle?"

She clears her throat and licks her lips. The action has me growling with longing, yearning to sink into her heat and not stop until I've had my fill and my cock can no longer stand firm. I lean in to nibble on her bottom lip, coaxing her to let me have more of her. I want to taste her needy pussy so badly it makes my mouth water thinking about it.

"The other guy is still up front, and the employees will be here soon. They can't see him knocked out."

"Damn it," I grumble, and she nods, agreeing with my frustration of having to stop. The other time I had her like this we were interrupted by Ace. Now it's these stupid Iron Fists. I push another kiss to her lips and promise, "This isn't over."

She hums, with a teasing smirk. "Bossy biker, I'm not that easy." Her hand trails down my abs to brush over the hardness in my pants making its presence clearly known.

"You want it just as badly. Admit it," I murmur and adjust my dick after her teasing graze against my shaft.

Her gaze watches my every move full of longing. "You're right, I do." I groan, and she continues. "Doesn't mean I'm giving it up in a hallway with a knocked-out shithead at our feet."

With a huff, I openly admit, "I don't do romance." Ever the romantic, I should shut my fucking mouth if I want any semblance of a chance with this woman. I just can't seem to do it whether it makes shit harder for me or not.

She shrugs. "Neither do I, although I'm not one to turn down chocolate syrup, or in your case, some peanut butter. If that's your version of romance, anyway."

"Fuck," I breathe the curse. She had to bring up the peanut butter, and that makes me think of her fucking tongue and how it swirled around my finger when we had those pancakes. I want her head bobbing below me as she works peanut butter clean from my cock. God, the thought of it has me groaning low in my throat.

"Come on, cupcake. Time to grab this idiot from the front. You should probably call your MC brothers."

"I can shoot them a text. now show me where this other guy's at." The sooner they're out of my way, the sooner I can get back to touching her.

12. Buckle Up, Buttercup.

-Pinterest Meme

CHEVELLE

The Oath Keepers got here just in time to get the other bikers out of the way before my employees, and the other racers showed up. That would've been a big mess had any of them noticed an unconscious man lying around. Hopefully, no other trouble comes our way. I can't be up front to keep any other Iron Fists from getting in tonight since I plan on racing.

I can, however, warn my crew to keep a look out for them, but I won't have them turn the Iron Fists away. I'd be too afraid for their safety. Those one-percenters don't mix well with being told no, and I refuse to be the cause of them getting hurt, or worse, killed. My own safety is one thing; I'm more than capable of defending myself. My employees, however, are just normal everyday people with families at home.

The only way I knew to wait at the back door with the other biker for help was because Viking sent me a text letting me know Mercenary was on his way. I can't believe the stubborn man didn't listen to his president. I told that guy to take control of his brother. I won't let a man dictate whether I race or not. I know Mercenary will put up a fuss when he sees me line up on the track tonight. I don't need the distraction or any of the other racers witnessing me allow a man to have a say around here. They have to know I run this show.

On the plus side of these idiots scoping out The Pit or whatever they were doing, it was a decent distraction. Viking said Mercenary was not pleased hearing I'd called, so the unconscious guys took his focus off me for the time being. I have no idea what the Oath Keepers are doing with all these unwanted bikers they're taking off my hands, and I want it to stay that way. The less I know, the better. I've never been a snitch, but like I said, the less I'm aware of, the easier not to slip up.

Ace steps up beside me. "All drivers are ready. They listened to your suggestion and didn't bring their race vehicle on the property until thirty minutes ago, and I've had someone watching them all in case one of the drivers needs to leave for a minute or whatever."

"Good, thank you."

"I didn't like the last race any more than you. I don't want you hurt, Chevy."

Smiling gratefully, I nudge his shoulder like I would if he were an older brother. He's always reminded me of what it'd be like to have one. "All right, let's get started. The sooner we can erase the last race from their minds, the better." I nod toward the stands, and he agrees.

"I'll signal the music."

"And I'll line up."

I quickly peer around and hightail it to my ivory painted nineteen sixty-eight Dodge Charger RT. It's been a few weeks since I drove him and it's his turn to have a little fun on the track. Mercenary's distracted and hasn't had a chance to dig into me again about racing tonight. Not that I'd listen to him if he tried—he doesn't own me and never will. The man will learn that I do whatever the fuck I want to.

"Flower" by Moby begins to play through The Pit speakers, and a smile takes over. I haven't heard this song in forever, and I love to race to it. There's something about the beat; it's made to be listened to in a fast car.

I slide into the matching buttery soft leather seats—the beautiful chiffon color complementing the beast of a car and slide the key in the ignition. My stomach flutters excitedly as I twist the key and he thunders to life. He sounds like a grouchy old bastard pissed off for being woken up. No worries, he'll be purring like a kitten once I give him a little gas.

Pushing the link'd button, the stereo inside syncs to the speakers blaring through the dome. At the roar of my engine, Mercenary's gaze pins on me, and boy does he look furious. I send him a little wave with my fingers and romp on the gas. The car fishtails before straightening for the line. It's been too long since I drove him. He seems a bit angry with me.

"It's okay, baby," I soothe and rub my hand along the ebony dash. Yes, I talk to my vehicles. Anyone in their right mind who loves their cars speaks to them.

The other three vehicles I'll be going against roll up, lining up around my spot. My car rumbles, just waiting to be set free to whip some ass. The song changes, and right on cue, the passenger door swings open, a large body sliding in. I'm so focused on the sound of my engine and exhaust, gearing up for my race that it takes a moment to grasp that he's right next to me.

My mouth drops open. "What the hell? You can't be in here!" I yell as the engines around me drown out the music. I'm racing against some experienced fuckers, and I don't need Mercenary distracting me right now.

He whips the belt across his chest. "Bullshit. You want to race when it's not fucking safe, then I'm riding with you."

"You're like two hundred fucking pounds, man, get out!" I yell, pissed and glare at his stone cold blue eyes. The smoke slowly creeps up, surrounding the vehicles and cocooning us as various racers smoke out their tires.

My foot presses on the gas, my engine roaring in response as the car shakes, wanting to be let loose. It's to warm the engine up, and it also helps play a part in psyching out my opponents. They know I race to win, no matter what I drive, but Mercenary is adding unnecessary weight to my ride. It's one of the reasons I don't have a massive sound system in my car. I do without big speakers, and in return, my car weighs less than the others.

"I'm not moving, so if you want to win, I suggest you pay attention."

"I'm so kicking your ass for this shit," I swear as the song changes to 'Zombies' by The Cranberries and the race begins.

I let up the brake, and the car's so powerful the front end lifts off the ground. All of my cars do, and I freaking love the feeling of immense horsepower at my fingertips. Mercenary's arms shoot out with a curse, one holding the dash, the other gripping the oh shit handle like it's life or death for him. An evil smile takes over as we slam back to the ground and the Charger shoots forward as if the devil's nipping at its heels.

My rear tires squeal even though I already ran the set of rubber earlier and Mercenary shouts, "How is this legal?"

I scream at the distraction. "Shut the fuck up, cupcake!" I shift gears and swerve to the right, blocking the clown coming up behind me. I have to concentrate. It's the main reason I always win—not the car, but because I pay attention, I don't get sidetracked. I'm sure he growls in response, but I shut everything out and race. There's five grand on the line, and I don't plan on losing it.

We head around the last turn, and one of the cars bumps my rear end. I swerve, nearly losing control, but keep my cool as I sail over the finish line. As we pull to a stop, I leap out of my car and fly for the other driver.

He's just climbing out when I lay into him. My fist flies at his face in spite of his carelessness. We have rules in place to keep drivers as safe as possible. It's already dangerous enough driving at that speed on an enclosed track around so many people, but this asshole wants to rub me? "You hit my damn car!" I yell and throw another punch.

He reciprocates with a punch of his own. He has enough muscle behind it, I see stars for a moment, and then I hear a roar. I'm thrown to the side as two hundred pounds of pissed off alpha makes ground beef of the dude's face that just hit me. I stand there, shocked as I witness why the guy I've come to push around without a second thought is called Mercenary. The man wails into the other guy with such speed and strength the asshole's knocked out within moments of it even beginning.

Odin and Torch hurry to him, each grabbing for the mammoth of a man, taking hits in the midst of pulling him off the unconscious body below him. They eventually wrestle him off, but it's no easy feat. Breathing deeply, I stare, wide-eyed. Mercenary could've easily killed the other driver.

I lost my temper, and he fed off of it, going ballistic. The man is raw power, ready to dole out punishment. It makes me think that when I flipped him before, that he touched me with kid gloves. The animal in front of me could've killed me that day if he'd wanted to. Instead, he pulled my hair and stared at me like he wanted to fuck me. Jesus Holy Wow Christ.

Ace is by my side the next time I blink. "You okay?"

I swallow and nod. "My cheek is throbbing, but it won't hurt too badly until my adrenaline wears off."

"You could've wrecked, had that asshole hit you off to the side, and you spun out."

"I know. I was so pissed I couldn't stop myself."

He nods. "I figured." Our gazes lock on the rear of my Charger. "At least the car's good." He's right, there's paint on the bumper, but it'll buff off.

"I love old cars," I sigh in relief. I would've been even madder had it been dented up.

"Me too," he agrees. "What are you going to do with him?" He gestures to the guy on the ground.

"Someone drag him out back and drive his car out too."

"You want him banned?"

I nod. Whoever drives his car outside will spray paint "banned" across both sides of his car. He'll be pissed, but he's lucky I let him keep his car after breaking the rules. I should be a real bitch and send it to a chop shop.

I make my way to a panting Mercenary. My palm finds his cheek, his crazed gaze finding mine. "You okay, big guy?" I swear he grows an extra foot taller and wider when he gets into a fight. He was massive the last time the Iron Fists came to my office too.

"I'd be better if you'd listened to me and parked the damn car."

I roll my eyes and Odin interrupts us. "Prez wants you at the club, right now."

"I'm racing next," Mercenary argues.

Odin shakes his head. "Forget the race. Head back before more shit hits the fan."

"You told him I was in the car with Chevelle?" His brow furrows.

"I had to; he told me if you tried to stop her from racing to call him immediately."

"Fuck!"

We've caused a big enough scene; I can't do more drama without losing business. Last week it was a bomb, this week a near wreck, and then an all-out brawl. We need to get out of here so the others can race.

162

"Hey, Titus," I call to one of the workers on the track. "Park my Charger in his spot, please."

"Okay, boss." The kid nods and hops into my car eagerly.

"Let's go to the club, Mercenary."

"No, I'm racing and staying here to keep you safe."

"Fine." I shrug and start walking to my other cars. "Then I'll go by myself and tell Viking all about tonight," I threaten and quicken my steps.

"You're a fucking tattle tale now? Is that how you're going to play this?" I hear him behind me, his voice getting closer. I know he's chasing me down, his fast stride easily catching up.

I hop in my Chevelle and push my door lock down. He watches me on my side and with a huff, rounds to the passenger side, sliding in and slamming my door.

"I hit that fucker back there because he touched you! None of it would've happened if you'd listened to me, damn it!" he grumbles, and I start the Chevelle, heading for the bay in the back. Ace will take care of everything here for the time being.

13. A king only bows down to his queen.

- 100XSUCCESS

MERCENARY

I can't believe she went against everything I warned her about and decided to race. She's so damn stubborn. The woman has me vibrating with anger. I can't believe she hit that fucker rather than letting me take care of it for her. I would've killed him had my brothers not wrestled me off.

"You're infuriating, the most difficult damn woman I've come across."

"You're no spring picnic yourself, you know. You come into my life, demanding to take over. It won't happen with me, I don't need to be smothered."

"If I want to take over, you'd know it, and it'd fucking happen." Smothered my fucking ass, I've stayed so far back when it comes to being all up in her shit. She thinks this is bad, she hasn't seen smothered yet. Once this bitch is mine, she won't be able to walk five feet away without me knowing about it.

"Oh really? Is that what you think?" she huffs, her cheeks turning a sweet shade of pink with her frustration. "Clearly you didn't catch my drift when we first met or every day since then!"

"I caught it, trust me. You need me to spank your ass and fuck you until you break."

Chevelle's gaze flashes to me. "I *let* you spank me." Her eyes train back on the road in front of us. She's driving way too fast, still pumped up from the race and the fight no doubt.

Arguing with her only increases my heart and turns me on. "And you were soaked from it. You need to be fucked, Chevelle, and hard. You need to feel what it's like to have a real man between those thighs and in your life."

She snorts and my face flushes, not being able to show her right this second. My cock wants to be buried in her so badly it's on my damn mind constantly. Prez was right about me not being able to focus. Especially when she gets like this, all wound up and gorgeous and shit. *Fuck.*

"You won't break me, Mercenary," she declares, and I respond with a smug smirk, watching her breasts heave with each heavy breath she draws in and exhales.

"The hell I won't. When this is over and done with, you'll be begging me for more. I'll have my cock in you so deep you won't be able to speak, and when I finally *let* you, it'll be *my name* on that tongue."

"Does your ego have no bounds?" She shakes her head.

If she only had a clue—my ego's bigger than this damn car. I've had way too many women to not be confident when it comes to my cock and the female anatomy. Women love me when I'm eight inches deep. I may not be able to bend her to my will right this moment, but I can tease her a bit.

Turning in my seat, I reach across with my right hand, tweaking her nipple.

She sputters, her mouth dropping open as a deeper blush spreads across her cheeks and chest. "What are you doing? I'm driving!"

"Exactly...and I'm doing whatever the hell I want to," I grumble, and my left hand takes over, plucking her now erect nipple. My right hand lands on her thigh and the gas falters momentarily as I catch her by surprise. My palm slides up her thigh, closer to her core and her neck moves as she swallows, trying to remain unaffected.

"Mercenary?" It leaves her with a breath, the sound making my shaft grow.

"Right here, sweetie."

"You have to stop, I'm driving."

"Nah, don't think so." My palm stops at her juncture. I move my fingers and palm against her core, her back arching her chest against my other hand.

"Oh!" Chevelle moans. "I'm not fucking you. When I park this car, this stops," she threatens, and I continue to rub her until she's a turned on, whimpering mess. "You should've trusted me back there," she mumbles, her thoughts jumping back to earlier and then back to the present.

"If you want my trust, Chevelle, you'll have to give some first. And this body is aching; it needs me to fuck it. You want me just as much, whether you admit it or not."

"That's not how this works, Mercenary."

We arrive at the club far too soon in my opinion. I was enjoying being in the position to drive her crazy and her not being able to stop it without pulling the car over. She brings the vehicle to a stop, and we both hop out, rounding the front until we meet in the middle. Chevelle believes she's in control. She's the most infuriating woman when she attempts to fight me for dominance.

"I'm the fucking alpha, Chevelle. I run this shit," I declare with a harsh growl, glowering down into her horny stare. Those eyes of hers are swirling with emotion. She's pissed and turned on all at once, and boy is she the sexiest fucking woman I've ever seen when she gets like this.

"Others may put up with your Neanderthal ways, but I don't. I'm in control," she hisses. "That back there was bullshit. You weren't being fair!"

Another growl rumbles my chest. "In control?" I ask with a deadly undertone lacing my voice as I lean in, my nose a hair's breadth away from touching hers. "Fuck control! I take it. I own it. You want control, pet? Too fucking bad, 'cause I bend it to my fucking will. *You* will bend."

My hand flies to her toned bicep, yanking her to me like a rag doll; my other grabs her high ponytail and wrenches her head back. She moans at my dominant behavior, wanting to possess every ounce of the control she *thinks* she has. "You're mine," I declare and slam my mouth to hers.

I take the kiss. Stealing whatever bit she'll offer me of herself. I have to own her. I need this woman on my cock too fucking badly to be gentle with her. Our teeth clash, both of us strung so tightly and wanting to dominate the other.

I hold her so tightly to me that she can barely move. Her breath's come out ragged as she attempts to catch her breath in the midst of me owning her mouth with mine. Nails that she's bitten down to the skin try to rake over my chest, dragging me to her and pushing me away all at the same time. Chevelle fights the desire we're both so desperately filled with. She calls to my body like none other—it's the type of craving that'll make a man lie, cheat, and kill to possess it.

169

Wrenching back from her blissful lips, I draw in a few deep breaths, and in the next blink I'm grabbing her other arm and slamming her back down onto the hood of her car.

"I'm not yours," she chokes out, glaring daggers at my mouth. The mouth that just stole a kiss from hers, that branded her until her lips reddened and swelled to a delicious pout.

"Keep telling yourself that. I've already decided you're mine and I take whatever the fuck I want."

She burns for me; I can see it. Her nipples are hard through the thin tank top material, her cheeks flushed. My nostrils flare as her scent hits me. Her pussy is wet and ready, and I've barely even begun to touch her. It's enough to cloud my vision as I jump forward, taking over every ounce of her space. Shoving her up farther on the hood, her body's sprawled against the warm metal. She's angry, needy, and absolutely beautiful.

Without another thought, my hands yank her tank top, ripping the thin cotton in half. Flinging the barrier to the side, her tits left exposed. Her breasts heave as she draws in a stunned breath at my so-called Neanderthal ways.

"You tore my fucking shirt!" Her hands fly toward my chest, shoving me hard once and then grabbing my shirt to yank me closer. I bet her panties are soaked from me taking over and I can't wait to find out if I'm right.

My mouth laps at her breasts as soon as I see them. My lips switch from one to the other, wanting to have them both at the same time. I squeeze the melons together to my delight. She has the perfect set of tits, just big enough if I squeeze them a bit she has a sexy line of cleavage. My cock's so fucking hard, if I'm not careful I may dent the hood of the car.

I make her wither and groan in delight as I suck and nip at her divine chest, before beginning my trail lower. Her hands find my spikey hair, gripping the locks between her fingers to tug. My tongue skirts along her tummy, dipping into her navel. She shudders at the movement, enlisting a primal growl from me. *I must have her. Own. Conquer.*

My fingers find the button and zipper of her shorts, plucking and tugging until the obstacle's free. I can't move fast enough when it comes to Chevelle. I have the insatiable need clawing through my veins to pound into her pussy until she gives in to me and swears to obey me in every way.

"That feels so good, Mercenary. You better stop. I'm not some cheap whore you pick up whenever you want. We fuck when I say so."

"You better shut that fucking mouth, Chevelle," I grumble. "I'm fucking you. Now." At that, my hands close around the waist of her shorts, tugging them over her muscular thighs. She can pretend to fight me, but I know the truth. I can feel her practically vibrating with desire under me. Her scent is all around, utterly intoxicating.

I pop the button on my jeans and shove them down enough for my cock to spring free, eager to feel her.

"You couldn't keep up with me," she claims, and my fingers claw at the scrap of material she wears as panties. She's constantly challenging me, seeing how far she can push. She'll learn I'm not breakable; she can shove me, but I always push right back.

I'm too far gone. My cock strains, craving her as she enrages and goads me on. My hands shred her underwear into pieces, leaving behind red marks on her skin in my impatience. "Keep up?" I ask as I lick my lips, my gaze trained on her glistening folds. "You are so goddamn wet. Your juices are dripping on the fucking car."

At that, I wrap my arm around her lower back and slide her to me, impaling my cock into her at the same time. She cries out at the surprise intrusion. "Fuck! you're huge!" Her shocked irises find mine.

"You thought I was playing? I told you I would own you, pound this pussy until you've surrendered."

Her mouth falls open as I jerk my hips back and drive into her even deeper this time. "Oh shit. You were telling the truth about the eight inches."

"That's right, Chevelle. I'm the fucking alpha. I have the cock filling your pussy. Tonight, you succumb to me, sweetie."

"You're the alpha?" She gasps on another thrust. "Fuck me for it then. Show me." She leans up, pinning me with her burning gaze.

At that, all I can do is drive into her harder and roar. It feels like all I do is growl around this bitch. She drives me crazy inside, makes me want to pound my fist to my chest and own every piece of her.

"Faster," she orders.

At her command, I slam her back against the hood again. She starts to lean up, but I hold her still by wrapping my free hand around her throat. She wants to move then she'll stop breathing. Chevelle will learn I'm in control even if I have to break her to do it.

My other hand holds tightly onto her hip as I thrust forward, attempting to shove my cock so deep into her she feels it in her throat. With each pop of my hips, her tits shake, my gaze trained on each bounce. "Why do you have to be so difficult? I swear to Christ if you don't learn, I'm going to start shoving my cock in that pretty mouth every time you fuckin' speak!"

"You want pliant? Go find some timid bitch who's scared of you," she yells back, as my hand squeezes her delicate throat at her words.

"If you were smart, you'd be scared." My mouth descends on her nipple again, biting until she whimpers.

"Fuck. You."

"You are," I rasp, driving deep enough that her next cry has her hands flying to my chest, grabbing for anything she can reach.

"Hurt?" I ask cockily as I continue to take her body with wild abandon. There's nothing like the whimpers and moans from a woman as I fuck her to stroke my ego. This chick just so happens to be as crazy as I am, which is a first. I've come across plenty of women who claim to be alpha, but none of them hold up to that title. Chevelle is an entirely different breed. She was made for me.

She's the type that has you going back to the beginning, back when it was important to seek out the strongest mate to breed. You searched to find the one that could bare your children that would be healthy and strong—someone to compliment your own attributes. A male was supposed to hunt, to provide for his family and to keep them safe. It was his job to protect and provide and the woman's to have his children, to continue his blood line...to worship him.

Chevelle has me wanting to prove to her that I'm the strongest mate she'll ever come across. That I can offer her what she needs, to claim her and make her mine. What is it with men and wanting to own pretty things? To possess them so another can't have it? I want to lay my claim on Chevelle, so no one even dares to fucking look at her.

"Please," she begins to beg, her pussy squeezing my cock harder and harder as her climax builds. I love hearing the surrender in her voice as she gets closer to bliss.

"You mine?" The question escapes before I can push the thought back down and what it means exactly. I don't care about the technicalities; I care about her pussy wrapped so tightly around my cock that it wants to explode.

"Oh, please," she whimpers.

"Say it, now." I squeeze her throat, stealing her air as I stole her kiss earlier. Her pussy pulses in response and I loosen my grip.

"Yes," she croaks on the verge of spiraling into bliss, but it's still not good enough.

"Are. You. Mine." My demanding voice rises with every word and each plunge into her core.

"Fuck! Yes, I'm yours, you selfish bastard!" she finally admits on a lurid exclamation, and a raging desire unlike any I've ever felt before shoots through me. My hips pound so deftly into her that the sound of our flesh meeting echoes into the night.

"Say my fucking name."

"Mercenary," she chants loudly. "I'm yours, Mercenary. Please let me come." I release her throat completely, my hand falling to pinch and pull her nipple and it sets her off like fireworks on the Fourth of July.

She screams through her orgasm, into the black night. My own mounting pressure erupts at her declaration, and my cock pumps my come into her waiting heat. A few easy thrusts and I'm spent for the moment. I'll want her again in a few minutes, I know it. She's like a drug, and one hit is not going to be enough to satiate my desire.

Holding still in her, my dick throbs, pumping every last drop I have. She remains laying on the hood, covered in her sweat, panting and staring up at the sky. I think it's the most beautiful look I've seen on her. Like this, covered in my scent and utterly content from me giving her a good fucking.

Cheering and clapping comes from off to the side, and we both turn to find my club brothers lined up against the front of the clubhouse. They just got one hell of a show. I wonder how long they were watching us and if Chevelle's going to lose her shit? However long, it must've been for a while as they continue to wolf whistle and make brash comments.

14.

MERCENARY

"Damn Merc! I'd say the bitch is yours!" Saint calls, a shit eating grin plastered on his pretty boy model face. I'm sure he loves this since he knows I think his ol' lady is fine as fuck. I figured he and Sinner would've left to find Ruger already, but apparently not.

The brothers make their way to us, and I pull my dick free from Chevelle's tight center, tucking it back into my pants. She stays rooted in place, my come dripping from her slit, breasts still heaving as she sits up. "Fuck," Chevy whispers for my ears only. Her irises flick over the approaching men. She remains calm though thanks to her orgasm and natural confidence.

She may not care if these guys see her naked, pussy still full of my come, but I'm not thrilled with it. She's hot as hell with clothes on, naked is even more of a reason for them to try and get in her pants. I set my cut down on the hood and tug my shirt off then pull it over Chevelle's head. Every bit of me wants my cut over the bitch too, showing the world she belongs to me and no one else.

Chevelle catches on to my movements, covering her up and sticks her arms through the holes, pulling the fabric over her. When she stands, the material comes all the way down to her knees. The sight causes my dick to harden all over again, seeing her in my shit, knowing she's naked underneath it.

Putting my cut on, I fist bump each of my brothers as they step up, standing around the car. They each wear various amused smirks and grins. Viking flicks his sturdy gaze over Chevelle and then it lands on me. "Quite a show you two put on," he observes.

I shrug.

"Want to fill me in on what went down tonight?" he asks, and Chevelle stares at me, biting her bottom lip, looking all cute and shit.

"She decided to race and then punch the other driver."

My brothers snicker and give her props.

I continue, unfazed. "The guy hit her back, so of course I beat him into a coma. And then she had the audacity to get pissed at me over it. We were arguing, so I had to show her who the fuck was in control."

She snorts, and my arctic gaze turns stormy, landing on her. She quiets with wide eyes. I doubt she's scared. I'm confident she knows I'd never hurt her. That doesn't mean I won't hold her down and fuck her in front of the club again until she admits that I'm right.

The guys all nod, their faces in agreement. Viking shrugs. "Makes sense. You two finished out here?" He gestures to the car and Chevelle's cheeks redden. I doubt she'll ever be able to look at that car again without remembering us on that hood.

"For now," I agree and grab her hand in mine. She pauses to swipe her shorts, and we walk hand in hand behind the Prez to the clubhouse. The brothers trail us as we enter the bar. "I'll show you the bathroom." I tug her off to the side.

We cross the dark bar. The light's at a low, comfortable level and various TVs all turned on to sports channels but muted, and rock music drifts throughout the room. Once we get to the hallway leading to our personal rooms, I open a door off to the right that has the public bathroom. She flashes me a grateful smile and hurries inside. I head back to swipe a clean shirt from my room and then back to pull out a stool at the bar next to Viking. He needed to talk to me; hopefully, it's not too serious, and it can be handled right here.

"O said you wanted to speak with me."

"Yeah, he'd told me what went down and then hung up when you started fighting. I wanted to get you out of there before you were arrested and ended up in jail. I heard you liked to knock some skulls around from your old Prez, not that you were always about to get locked up for your temper."

I shrug and signal for Chaos to get me a beer. "Same thing."

"Hardly. What's up with you and Chevelle? Is shit getting serious?"

"Well, it wasn't before, but after that fight and fuck, I suppose so."

"We take claiming in front of the club serious. If it's not a club whore, then we're expecting to be welcoming a new ol' lady. You know the club laws here."

I agree. "I do." I had to know them and take an oath before they'd even vote on me transferring to this charter. Chicago's laws were similar but no public claiming was ever mentioned. I guess these Texans like to watch their brothers fuck their women. I can see the attraction to it after witnessing Saint and Sinner fuck Jude in church. Holy hell, that was hot.

"So, we treat her as an ol' lady then. She'll get your property patch, but listen carefully..." He trails off, and I give him my full attention.

"If you plan to keep fucking the club sluts around here, you keep Chevelle away. We don't do drama; I'll boot her out on her ass if she comes in here kicking all the club sluts' asses and stirring up trouble with the brothers."

"I won't be fucking any of the whores again. Chevelle's all I want."

He nods. "Good. Most of us prefer to take the faithful route. That being said, though, the club sluts will come on even stronger at first. They seem to think when we put a property patch on our bitch that they have a chance. They don't ever realize that they never had a chance in the first place."

"I'll keep it in mind. Maybe if Chevy sees them like that it'll get her to come to her senses quicker."

"Another thing…when we claim the women, well…"

I stare, waiting, wondering what the hell has the Prez at a loss for words. He's not much of a talker, but he has me thinking that what he has to say must be top secret or something of that nature. Do they grow tails or something? I mean, what the fuck?

"I've been told they go, ah, a little cum crazy."

I nearly choke. That was the last thing I was expecting to hear from him. "Excuse me?" He has to be fucking with me.

Viking's tongue flicks against one of his canines before grunting and taking a gulp of his drink. He sets the tumbler on the bar, a smirk taking over as he thinks over something. "When I claimed my ol' lady, I pinned the bitch down and fucked her in the middle of a bar for taunting me."

My eyes grow wide. It's hard to imagine, Princess, his woman, seems too feisty to let that go over smoothly. "And Princess?"

"Oh, she was fucking pissed being claimed out in the open. I'd barely spoken a handful of words to her beforehand."

My eyebrows must be to my hairline at this point hearing all of this come out. "You started the public claiming?"

He nods. "She slapped the shit out of me in front of the entire bar too."

A grin breaks free as I attempt to hold back a laugh from spilling. Her slapping him is something I can definitely see happening. My Prez is a brute, though; I don't see him putting up with it.

"Anyhow, that's not where I'm going with this. My point is, after the slapping incident, she went a little nuts. She basically jumped on my cock, and I fucked her for four days relentlessly. The only break I had was to eat and shower."

"Damn, sounds like you locked her down."

He snorts. "I was dumb enough to think that at the time, but no."

"No?"

"No brother, I didn't lock her down. She locked me down. I was fucking hooked. I've taken her and planted my seed in that woman every damn day since."

"Doesn't sound so bad to me." I shrug.

He shakes his head, gesturing for Chaos to refill his glass before turning back to me. "It's not—at all. It's part of the reason why my loyalty has never wavered from her. I'm her king, and she's my queen. This doesn't have to do with me though. The way I saw you and Chevelle act and fuck, it just reminded me of myself when I first met my woman. Don't be surprised if Chevelle acts a little crazy and possessive for a while. It's all part of the effects of being owned properly."

"I can't believe I've never heard of this before." The concept is a touch crazy in itself. However, it would explain why my presence around Jude didn't do anything. Usually, I can have a woman eating from my palm if I wanted to, but she couldn't see past Saint and Sinner. I'm glad too. Clearly, I wasn't meant to have her. I just didn't know I'd be meeting Chevelle at the time. "I appreciate the info. I'll do what I need to."

"Good. Now we need to discuss those Fists that popped up earlier. What the fuck happened?"

I let him know everything Chevelle told me all the way up until Torch and Odin showed up to collect the unconscious men. When I finish disclosing what I know, she's making her way to us.

CHEVELLE

"Chevelle." Viking greets with a nod as I sit on the other side of Mercenary at the bar. Every man in this place looks like a goddamn tank. I'm not normally very nervous around men since I can usually kick their asses, but this place has me off balance. There's so much testosterone floating around, I swear you can taste it. Not only are the bikers in the Oath Keepers the size of mountains and full of muscles, but they're all gorgeous in their own unique way.

"Hello, Viking," I greet, feeling a bit more confident now that I've had a chance to clean up and put my shorts back on.

The MC brother behind the bar approaches me. He's built like a linebacker and fits in here with the rest of them. I grin reading over his name patch—*Chaos*. If I was a biker, I'd definitely want a road name like that.

"Cool name." I nod to the right side of his cut, and he offers me a grin in return. He's older than the rest of the guys around this place but super good-looking. I don't know what they put in the water or beer here, but it's a club full of ridiculously hot, broody, outlaw bikers. I wonder if you have to be hot in order to wear the Oath Keeper patch. It wouldn't surprise me, at this point.

"Thanks, peach, can I get you something to drink?"

"Sure, I'll take a seven-seven if you have it."

"That's vodka and seven up, mixed with ice, right?"

My grin drops as my eyes scan over the bar, checking if they have the liquor for the drink in stock. "It's Seagram's with 7 Up." You'd think he'd know how to make the simple drink; he's the only one back there.

"Okay, no problem," he mutters and turns away to mix it.

"Thanks," I say, but I don't think he hears me; he seems to be in his own zone, concentrating on pouring the Seagram's.

Viking leans in. "He just started tending bar for us this week."

"Oh." I nod. Not that it matters to me. It was nice of him to ask if I wanted something since Mercenary didn't think to.

"Now, Chevelle, would you mind explaining to me your side of what all happened today? I need to know from you shooting those two guys all the way down to my brother here getting into a fight over you."

"Well, it wasn't over me, per se. I sort of jumped out of my car and threw the first hit. It wasn't until the guy punched me back that Mercenary lost it on him."

"The guy hit you?" Viking grumbles, stunned, his face turning from friendly to grim.

"Yeah. In his defense, I punched him first. The dick ran into my rear end when we were racing, and it's prohibited at The Pit, for safety. Needless to say, I was pissed."

"I understand." His stare lands back on Mercenary. "I thought you just popped off, being a loose cannon. My mistake brother. I would've done the same thing had I seen it."

Mercenary waves it off as no big deal and Chaos sets my drink down.

"Thank you," I repeat and take a long gulp through the straw. I'm suddenly thirstier than I'd originally thought, and the mixed beverage goes down smooth and refreshing. The racing, fucking, heat, and not to mention everything with the rival MC, has really been a lot to take in.

"You had the Iron Fists knocked out before you drug them inside, right? They didn't have a chance to touch you or talk to you?" Viking presses on, switching subjects quickly and I shake my head, reassuring him. "Good. I think it's probably safer if you two start staying here at night."

"But who will watch The Pit?" I sputter, caught off guard by his suggestion. He wants to protect me? What is it with these guys thinking I can't handle my own problems? Where were they when I was a ten-year-old living on the streets? I guess they were kids, but still, it would've been nice to have someone back then.

"I'll have my guys ride by randomly, and I'll also have a chat with the sheriff. See if he and his deputies are willing to drive by a couple times a night when he patrols as well. It won't be left abandoned or anything."

"You're friends with the sheriff? Aren't cops and bikers supposed to hate each other?"

"In most cases yes, but not in ours. Our alliance benefits the community, and the people's safety around here is important to all of us."

I turn to the silent man beside me; he's usually not this quiet. "And what do you think of all this?" He's normally first to voice his displeasure about anything to me, it seems.

"Viking's suggestion makes sense." His beefy arm falls across the back of my barstool. The heat coming off him so close it makes me shudder as the air conditioning kicks on, and the two temperatures clash against my skin at the same time. "The guys today make five Iron Fists disappearing, all while watching you."

His thumb trails over my spine, his sky-blue irises full of scorching heat as he gazes at me. "That's a large enough group to be noticed and to take out retaliation. If they decide to hit back, they'll rape and kill you, if you're lucky."

My mouth drops open. "If I'm lucky?" That's not my idea of luck, nor should it be anyone's.

He nods. "They could keep you alive and torture you for who knows how long, along with continued rape throughout the club members. Maybe after so much, they decide to sell you off so some twisted fuck can continue doing the same sort of abuse."

"Holy shit," I gasp and swallow the sudden lump in my throat. "How did I get in the middle of this and how can they get away with that?" The fingers on my right hand float toward him, eventually landing on his thigh, unconsciously seeking out his strength.

Viking interrupts. "You started making money. In our world when it comes to gambling, racing, drugs, that sort...if you make enough money, you get noticed. It was their fuck up believing that you're an easy target without someone watching your back."

"This is bad. All I wanted to do was run a clean track where people could relax, place some bets, drink a few beers, and watch races. I don't need these assholes coming and screwing it all up for me. And I damn sure don't like having my place bombed for their sick entertainment."

"Well, it may take some time, but we're working on getting rid of this problem. Luckily you'll be able to benefit from it as well."

"By staying here, do you mean with cupcake?" I tilt my head toward the broody biker at my side.

"Cupcake?" Viking snorts out a chuckle and Mercenary grumbles while shooting me an unamused side-eye.

I nod, glancing at the both of them. Mercenary's the only man I call cupcake. At first, I did it to piss him the hell off, and it worked flawlessly. It quickly morphed into me calling him cupcake 'cause he was pretty sweet to me when he wanted to be. And now, well...it's because his cocks as thick as a damn cupcake. The fucker's got a massive sized dick. I could stuff myself with it all the damn time and be peachy keen.

"Listen, doll, Merc here," he gestures to the man in question, "claimed you out front. He essentially made you his ol' lady since he fucked you in front of the entire club and then made you admit that you're his."

I blow out a breath, pretty confident I know enough biker lingo to understand what he's getting at. I ask anyway, just to be certain. "What does that mean?"

"You belong to him; you're a part of this club."

I jump to my feet, my thoughts confirmed and my fist slams into Mercenary's rock-hard bicep. "You ass!"

He stands, towering over me. "Woman, don't make me take you over my knee."

I sputter, my cheeks growing warm with my irritation at this bossy-ass man. "You're off your damn rocker if you think I'll put up with your macho shit!" I yell, and he moves like a freaking ninja, catching me off guard. I'm good at defending myself when I'm expecting it, but Mercenary whips me up in his solid arms, hiking me to hang over his wide shoulder. I curse him loudly, and his brothers throughout the bar snicker. His hand lands on my ass—hard.

"Shut the fuck up, Chevelle!" he commands, and his MC brothers laugh even louder at his disgruntled boom. He grumbles, "I'll catch you later Vike, obviously this bitch has been without my cock for too long. She gets mouthy; I have to go fix it."

"Remember what I said," Viking responds ominously, and I flash my middle finger at Mercenary's back. He can't see me, but it still counts.

I let out my own growl, hanging upside down but I have a feeling that with all the noise in the bar, that I sound more like a pissed off kitten as Mercenary stomps away, taking us to his room.

15. **Happiness is an inside job.**
Don't assign anyone else that
much power over your life.
- HPLYRIKZ.COM

MERCENARY

I feel the woman at my side stir, rousing me further from my deep, sated sleep. We're both still naked from a long night of me proving just how much she really is mine. Pulling her closer, I line my cock up and sink into her from behind.

I'll never have enough of her or her body; the woman keeps me on my toes. I'm quickly learning the only way to keep her temper from lashing out at me is to keep her satisfied with my cock. Not that I mind in the slightest. I'm getting to know every inch of her delectable body, and a pleased Chevelle is even sexier than a pissed off Chevelle.

"Mmm, again?" she mumbles sleepily, and I push farther, sinking deeply into her warm sheath.

"As much as possible," I groan against the back of her neck, pushing her hair out of my face, and breathe her in. "You smell so damn good. Like rain and springtime."

With a quiet laugh, she replies huskily, "I smell like your soap."

"I know, and I like how my soap smells."

She snickers, and I find myself grinning like an idiot against her skin. She asks, "No more fucking this morning?"

"I'm tired. Besides you said you were sore the last time," I rumble and slowly plunge into her again, my hand skirting over her ribs, stopping to cup her full, heavy breasts.

"Mmm, I should've believed you about the eight inches thing. I thought you were full of it. Turns out I'm full of it."

"You're still chirping about that?" I groan as my cock throbs, encased in her welcoming core.

"It's impressive."

"You needed to be fucked badly, sweetie. Your pussy belongs on my cock." I nip at her neck, pulling my hips back to sink into her again, driving my pleasure on. "Fuck, you're good for my ego." Reaching down I seek out her clit. We're old friends by now with how well I know that part of her body after merely one night.

Her head turns, burying her mouth in my pillow as she moans loudly and bites down. I've discovered just the way to touch her to make her beg me for more. I had her shooting off like the Fourth of July all night long. I'm not going to let her forget who's in control of her pleasure. I'll give it again and again until it's seared into her memory.

"You're gonna give it to me easily today then?"

Her bite on my pillow releases as she turns toward me as much as she can. "You got it easily last night too," she replies huskily, her voice laced with desire and sleep. Her leg hikes behind her, hooking over my thigh so I can go in deeper.

Bullshit. She fought me at every turn, making me work for her orgasms. She's stubborn, but I love a good challenge. "What can I say, your tight pussy likes me. It can't seem to get enough of my cock making it come."

Tucking my arm around her chest, I pick us up until I'm on my knees with her back pressed firmly against my chest. My free arm wraps around her, my palm landing on her core, grinding against her clit. My other plays with her breasts, squeezing and caressing her nipples with my fingertips. Her head falls back, resting on my shoulder. Her eyes stay closed with her mouth open, whimpering and moaning with my caresses.

My hips rock hers, my shaft thrusting into its own rhythm drawing a soft whimper from her. Her head turns to watch my face. "See, you shouldn't be able to move like that without breaking contact." The vixen smiles as she adds, "Eight inches *really* makes a difference."

"Nah," I rasp, turning to meet her lips. "You haven't been fucked properly before, that's all. Now you know that no motherfucker can do what I can." I take her mouth—morning breath be damned. I want to feel her tongue against mine. I was just kissing her hours ago, but it feels like it's been too long since we've had that contact. Her center tightens around me, already starting to milk my length as her climax draws near.

Breaking my hold on her breast, I use my arm for balance and lean us back until I'm lying flat on my back, impaling my cock into her heat in another position. Our mouths break apart in the move, and the change draws a deeper whimper from her. It's the perfect spot for me to play with her sensitive nub.

Her legs fall open, spread completely apart for me. Each leg rests across each of my thick, muscular thighs. Her long locks fall off the side of my shoulder, and I catch the scent of my shampoo as well. I like this, having my smell everywhere when it comes to Chevelle.

"Yes, oh yes," she cries deliciously.

I tilt her head farther off to the side and draw her skin between my lips to suck. She starts to shoot off me, but I hold her to me tightly. One hand continues to rub her pussy ruthlessly, the other wraps securely around her chest. My hand reaches up, gripping her neck in place, bracing her body to mine.

My moves coax the orgasm from her while I mark her so severely, the delicate tanned skin bruises with a deep purple hue. She'll wear it for the next few weeks to come before it fully disappears. Hell, something buried down wants me to bite her and draw blood. I've never had the feeling like that before, but I have this insatiable need for everyone to know she's taken. And to know death will follow them if they touch her.

Chevelle screams my name loudly, as the pleasure fully blooms over her body. I'm slowly wearing down her resolve toward me. Her tight, wet core squeezes my thickness so tightly, I follow her, pumping my own pleasure into her. Not only am I wearing her down, but I'm falling farther down the rabbit hole when it comes to her.

I hold her to me as I inhale and exhale a few times deeply, catching my breath and come down from the intense climax. The woman steals a piece of my soul each time I take her. Morning sex is one of my favorite things with her, no doubt. It's passionate, the pleasure reached easily, and so damn fulfilling.

When my arms finally fall away, she rolls off me to the side. Her hand flies to the spot showing the world that she's taken. "You marked me!" She hisses and glares. She can try to be pissed, but her eyes are still glazed over from how much she enjoyed it. The look makes me want to fuck her—hard this time.

"And?" My brow lifts, and I shrug, not fazed in the slightest bit at her irritation.

"I don't enjoy going around with hickeys on my neck. I have a business to run, and I'll look cheap."

"You're wrong," I argue. "You look like a woman who's been thoroughly enjoyed. A woman that's been claimed and has a man. A woman not to be fucked with by anyone with a cock in their pants."

She throws her arms up and huffs. "Men won't take me seriously, especially when it comes to cars. They'll see this mark and then look for a man, instead of taking me seriously."

"Then they'll find me right next to you, and I'll tell them you run The Pit."

"You don't understand, Mercenary. I don't want them to look for a man at all. They should see me in charge."

"Excuse me? Too fucking bad, because I'll be there and if any of them disrespect you, I'll knock their fucking teeth out."

"Some woman may fall at your feet hearing you proclaim that Tarzan crap, but I can take care of myself. I happen to enjoy doing the knocking out with my own two fists."

"Fucking shit, you're a pain in the ass."

She climbs out of bed and searches out her shorts and one of my shirts.

"What are you doing?"

"Going home." Chevelle sulks acting every bit of the flustered woman she was just claiming she isn't. She busily pulls her clothes on and covers up that beautiful body that I was lucky enough to get very acquainted with last night.

I jump out of bed and pull on a clean pair of jeans, garnering her attention.

"What are you doing?"

"Going with you." I shrug, gearing myself up for an argument. She'll no doubt have something to say especially right after I put a dark purple, huge hickey on her throat.

"Uh, no..." Chevelle trails off and shakes her head. She continues searching under random objects for her other shoe.

"You're not going back there alone. We don't know if there are Iron Fists waiting for you to return, and my bike's still there. We came in your car, remember?"

She sighs. "Fine, but we're stopping to get breakfast on the way, and since you want to be all manly, you're buying," she grumbles, and I yank on my shirt.

"Hard deal, but I think I can manage being forced to eat and pay." I tug on my boots, ignoring what I'm sure is an eye-roll directed my way.

We ended up going back to the taco shack to pick up breakfast burritos and thankfully the dumbass from yesterday wasn't working again. I don't think I could've handled seeing him eye my woman right after I've claimed her. I'd probably break his frail little beta male neck.

"Does it bother you that I don't cook?" Chevelle peers at me curiously. We're in the middle of eating after doing a search of The Pit. It was all clear, so now I'm enjoying nearly cold eggs, bacon, and cheese wrapped in a freshly made tortilla.

I shake my head. "Nah, why would I give a shit if you can cook?"

"Because I'm a woman." Her gaze flicks to the ground, and it has my own curiosity flickering to life. Is she actually nervous about what I think and over something so insignificant?

"That's pretty damn sexist," I mutter around my mouthful.

"I know, but most of the men I've come across tend to think something's wrong with me."

I swallow. "Well, for one, I'm not most men. And for another thing, they're fucking stupid. I'm used to eating out or my own cooking. I don't give a fuck if it's got to stay that way either. If I get too hungry, I could always just feast on your pussy."

She bites her bottom lip, her neck flushing at my suggestion and her gaze grows thoughtful. "What's your story, cupcake?"

I nearly choke on the new bite I've taken. "Uh, what?" It's so out of the blue that my mind spins over her question.

"What happened to make you decide to become a hard-ass biker? Don't take this the wrong way, but you're nothing like I'd expected when you first came to The Pit."

I swallow and offer her a smile. "Believe it or not, nothing."

"I'm not buying it," she admits, biting off her own mouthful of burrito.

"You don't have to, but it's true. I grew up with both of my parents, they're good people. I had a fun childhood, well, besides normal hormones and teenage shit. My family had enough money to get by, and I have an older brother who's a doctor."

"You're shitting me!" She stares at me, chewing slowly.

"Nope, I was fortunate in that department."

"Are you the black sheep or something, at least?"

I snort. "Why, because I ride a motorcycle, enjoy a good fist fight, like my liquor, and enjoy pussy more than the average feeble male?"

She nods, being completely honest with me.

"No, sweetie, my family loves me, rough and wild and all."

"You're lucky."

I nod. "I am. Got my first motorcycle in high school. I had a part-time job, and the bike was the first transportation I could afford. The rest is history. What about you?"

"Why do you want to know?"

"Well, besides the fact that you just bombarded me with all those questions? Because I want to know more about you than just your attitude and tight pussy."

Her cheeks tint, and I grin again. It's hard not to smile when she's sitting here all quiet and sweet, eating her breakfast and has made me come all night long. Usually, she tough as nails closed off Chevelle. I like her like this.

She tucks a long dark lock behind her ear and shrugs. "Not much to tell. I grew up on the streets."

"On the streets? Here?"

"No, in Houston. I ended up here by accident."

I nod, wanting to hear more. I want her to tell me everything there is to know when it comes to her. "And your family?"

"I have none." She shrugs, and I find it hard to believe that she's so unaffected. I may be a dick and all, but I still love my parents and sibling.

"Wait, you're an orphan." It's more of a statement than a question as the thought hits me.

She swallows. "Yes."

"Weren't you in foster care or something?" The thought of her alone all this time has my stomach in knots. No wonder she can easily be so closed off and cynical. It's how she's learned to protect herself on the inside.

"They tried, but I ran away."

"And no one caught you?" *My sneaky girl.* Can't say that surprises me. Chevelle likes to prove to everyone and herself that she needs nor wants anyone.

She clears her throat, growing tense. "No, I adapted." I can feel her closing off, so I drop it for now, but I still want to know.

"Damn, those burritos were good." I rub my hands over my stomach drawing her eyes to the taut, muscular area.

Her shoulders relax as she takes the subject change with ease. "I love that place. Eighty percent of their monthly sales probably comes from me."

"That's a lot of tacos, Chevy."

She smiles with a nod then stands and takes our trash, throwing it away. My eyes remain glued to her form as she sways in her own erotic strut she seems oblivious to. We were eating in the middle of the track. Random spot but this is where we ended up after searching the place, and with both of us starving decided to just sit and eat right on the track.

"So how did you get into racing?" I ask as she comes back, and I stand up. I don't know where we'll end up next, but I start walking beside her. Taking her hand in mine, she doesn't pull away, and like a fucking chick, I get all excited inside. Her pussy already has me whipped after only one night being buried in her wet warmth.

"I met this older man." My hard gaze finds hers, and she smiles. Shaking her head, she backtracks. "Think of him as a grandpa in a sense. He had a shop and fixed cars. He caught me begging near his place one night and told me if I helped clean up his shop, he'd buy me dinner. Being young and the promise of a full stomach, I jumped on the offer."

She takes a drink of her soda and continues. "His shop was trashed, but regardless, I cleaned it. The job ended up taking me nearly a week to complete, but each day as promised, he'd order a bunch of food. I'd eat until I was in a food coma and clean my ass off in return. He never asked me where I'd go at night, and before he'd have a chance to forget about me, I'd be out in front of the shop, first thing."

"Where *did* you go at night?" I interrupt to ask.

She sighs. "I was sleeping under a bridge near his business."

I make a sound in my throat, a cross between sadness and anger on her behalf. "Oh wow, you were serious about being on the streets." I didn't realize how much truth those words had held when she'd originally said them. No wonder she has it in her head that she has to do everything all on her own.

"Yes, anyway, he kept coming up with things for me to do. I was about twelve at that time, and eventually, his tasks switched to me helping him work on the cars that came in needing repairs. He taught me everything he knew about mechanics. After about two years of helping him, he started letting me work on cars by myself. Turned out, I could fix them faster than he could."

"I'm not surprised," I comment, and she smiles.

"Not only did he feed me, but he began paying me as well. A year before that, he'd let me start sleeping in the office at his tiny shop. It had a bathroom and a roof, so I was beyond grateful."

"You were fortunate he didn't take advantage of you."

"Trust me, I know."

That thought alone is enough to make me want to rip someone's head off. I'd kill them without a second thought if they touched her wrong in any way.

We get to her apartment, and she sits in the overstuffed chair. I take the edge of her bed. "He also owned a dirt track on the outskirts of Houston in this town called Katy. When I got old enough to drive, he taught me how in a race car around that track. A lot of the other drivers brought their car into the shop for mods, so I was already familiar with how a race car ran, how it ticked."

"Jesus, I bet you were a natural."

She nods with a wide smile in place. I've never seen her smile so bright; the beauty makes me swallow roughly.

"I started winning money racing one of his cars along with being paid to work in his shop. I was finally doing something real with my life. I had a purpose after so long of being filled with emptiness."

"So, what happened? Why'd you leave?"

The smile drops, her bottom lip trembles for a beat before she hides it. "He died."

"Sweetie, I'm sorry."

She nods, a sad smile taking the place of the tremble she wore moments prior. "His shop was sold by his lawyer as instructed in his will. I had some money to survive on at the time, but nothing to keep me afloat in Houston. Then his lawyer got ahold of me one day when things were looking down, and I found out the crazy old man had left everything to me."

"No shit?"

She nods. "He had a son somewhere that he knew nothing about and a bitter ex-wife that wouldn't speak to him. He'd told me I was like a daughter to him. I just never realized that he was serious, I guess. Anyhow, I immediately started looking for something...a small shop or whatever I could buy to make money and live a quiet life. I found The Pit. I bought my Chevelle and put the rest of the money I had as a down payment to the previous owner, and I've been racing to pay it off and fix it up each week since."

"Damn, Chevelle. I'm impressed. The man would be proud of you, no doubt."

"You are?" Is that hope in her eyes? She's like a kitten that scratches and hisses at first but then basks in attention shown to her by her owner.

"Hell yeah. You're a fighter in all senses. I suppose you learned to defend yourself from growing up like that then?" I can't believe this beautiful woman had such a hard life. I really am lucky with my family.

She nods. "You fight and adapt, or you die."

"You really are a badass," I mumble, and she pulls me down to the bed.

"Mmm, then it's my turn to have my way with you. Badasses get what they want." She smirks and pushes me against the comforter. She climbs over me, straddling my waist, giving me a perfect view of her beauty. She doesn't have to tell me twice. I'll gladly let her have her way with me.

16. If you're sad, add more lipstick and attack.

- Coco Chanel

CHEVELLE

The sounds of multiple motorcycles draw Mercenary's attention the next morning. He hops from the bed, nearly tripping in my sheet on his way to the window. We were supposed to go back to the club but wasted the day away talking about anything and everything. Then the night was spent filled with passion, wrapped in each other's bodies between the sheets on my bed.

"Shit, are you okay? What's going on?"

"I'm fine," he waves me off and mutters dismissively but not rude as he stares out the window to the parking lot below. "Fuck!" He curses as his eyes go wide at the scene. He flips around, scanning over every surface, not saying a word.

"What is it? You're freaking me out over here!"

"The fucking Iron Fists."

"So, shoot them!" I point to the tranq gun, my voice a higher note than normal.

"There's too many. Fuck!" Both hands rake through his spiked, inky hair in frustration. His stomach muscles clench as he paces, the movements offering up a delicious view of every toned inch. He's all strength and corded steel, strung tight at the impending fight the Fists will no doubt bring to The Pit.

"Can you shoot any of them or something?"

He tosses me his phone. "First number listed," he orders. "Dial it and tell them we need backup—quick—and to bring a fuck ton of it."

Fumbling with the phone, I do exactly as he says, watching as he points the tranquilizer gun and curses with each shot.

"O," a gruff voice answers the phone.

"Uh, Odin?"

"Yep, who's this?"

"It's Chevelle."

"Chevelle? You okay, chick?"

"Yes, there's no time to explain, but Mercenary says to bring a lot of backup to The Pit."

Merc hisses, a curse drawing my attention. He's fumbling with the gun. "What is it?" I ask, forgetting about Odin momentarily.

He flicks his gaze to me, not stopping his fingers from jiggling the metal. "I hit three, missed two and then this jammed." He briefly holds the gun up before turning his concentration back to it.

Odin yells through the phone, and I scramble to get it back to my ear. "What the fuck did he say? He shot three?"

"Yes, with the tranquilizer gun," I reply, not taking my gaze from Mercenary.

He grumbles. "Fucking shit, how many are there?"

I call to Mercenary, "How many are there?"

"I didn't stop and count the fuckers, tell him at least a dozen."

"Holy shit," Odin murmurs, yelling to people in the background. "Tell my brother to take you somewhere safe and wait us out. There's too many for you two to fight off. Your lives are too important to waste trying to stop the Fists. They're dangerous. If I thought you two could take them all without getting hurt, I'd say differently."

"Okay," I whisper, and he hangs up.

Mercenary pulls his Glock off the side table and checks to make sure it's fully loaded. I highly doubt his weapons aren't ever unloaded or not cleaned. He's too meticulous for any of that.

"He said for us to hide until they get here, cupcake."

He nods, yanking up his pants and tucking his feet into his boots. "Get dressed Chevy, quickly."

A loud boom shakes us, drawing my breath. I fall over my feet, hurrying out of bed toward my dresser and yank on the first thing I find. "What the hell was that?"

I want to scream but refrain. I'm not a screamer but whatever they blew up downstairs has me jittery. Mercenary's mood change has me a bit fidgety as well. I'm not used to him on edge except for when it comes to arguing with me. Even then, he's not as solemn as now.

"My guess is they couldn't get in, so they made a new door."

"Ugh!" The exclamation leaves me in a furious, unladylike growl. "I'm going to wrap each of their nuts around their throats and make them chew on them like fucking bubble gum!"

He smirks and tosses me the tranq gun after I slide my feet into a pair of Toms slip-on shoes. "Damn sweetie, you're mesmerizing when you're pissed." He gestures to the metal contraption. "Use that on any fucker who comes at you."

"I'd rather fight."

"If you want to make it safely out of here, you're going to have to trust me on this, Chevelle. I know you can fight, but what if there are three coming for you? Take out whoever you can safely, and then use your fists."

I huff but refrain from arguing with him. He knows this type of life better than I do. I got through the streets as a kid; I'll make it through a pack of rabid bikers.

"You'll wear yourself out too fast, and we may need to fight at some point to get out of here. If we can take some of the threat out with weapons, then let's use it to our advantage. I couldn't handle it if one of them hurt you. It'd be a bloodbath as I tore them limb from limb for it."

"I get it."

"Good, now where can we hide for the next twenty minutes or so where no one will think to look for us? We need to wait for backup to get here. I won't do anything to jeopardize your safety."

"Follow me." I gesture toward the door with him in tow. I lock it on our way out, and we walk down the hall between my office and my apartment, stopping in front of the maintenance door in the middle. "I need to lock my office."

"No, we don't."

"It'll be a distraction if they think we're locked in one of these rooms."

He has an 'ah-ha' moment and takes off jogging to my office. He opens the door and quickly locks it before closing it silently. "Locked." He tilts his head to me, coming to stand at my side.

I nod, remaining silent and open the janitor closet door. He rakes a hand through his spikey dark hair and then massages the back of his neck. "Locking three doors wasn't my idea of hiding out, sweetie."

"Shh!" I shoot him a glare and lock the thick metal maintenance door behind us.

He huffs, not so patiently watching me with a raised eyebrow. I head for the corner in the back right of the small ten-by-ten-foot room, lined with metal shelves and various cleaning supplies. I wave him to come near and point at the small square cut in the roof covered by thin wood. It's painted to match the ceiling, so you don't notice it right away when coming in the room.

"An attic?" he guesses.

I whisper, replying, "No, it's access for an electrician or to fix the dome, that sort of thing."

"Ah." He nods again, concentrating on listening for anyone coming up to this level.

"I'm too short; you have to pull the lip down."

He pulls me behind him and hops, easily touching the ceiling. His fingers skirt over the lip, missing. Taking a deep breath, he jumps again, this time finding purchase when his middle finger sinks into the one-inch-sized slot. He pulls the door all the way open, so it hangs toward us.

"I'll lift you." His hands go out to grip my waist, hefting me up. The man is definitely stronger than any other I've been with. He lifts me with such ease, and I can't help but think of what else he could do with my body like this if we were naked and not being hunted down by an irate MC club.

My hands reach for the opening, and I help to pull myself into the small entry area. Turning over, I sit on my butt and slide backward to give him some room. My hands come away covered in dust, and I quietly clap them together to remove the scratchy feeling. The area's a bit musty, the air stale like a closed-up attic. Good thing I don't have asthma — this would be an attack waiting to happen.

Good thing he enjoys pull-ups so much; a weaker man wouldn't make it. A few beats pass, and I'm about to pop my head back over when his hands appear, grasping the sides. He easily pulls himself up, high enough to readjust and get his elbows planted on the beams running along each side of the opening. This is just another randomly placed work out for him I suppose. Who needs a gym when you have ceiling beams to keep you fit?

He finds me. His brows jump, and I see he has a flashlight gripped in his mouth between his teeth. I go to reach for him to try and help pull him in, but he shakes his head. I reach for the flashlight and free it from his clenched teeth. He blows out a breath, his muscles bulging as he finishes lifting himself up. Once he makes it, he flips around, lies on his stomach, and reaches for the door, securing it to the ceiling before scooting back beside me.

"Good thinking," I praise, holding up the flashlight.

He nods, drawing in a deep, shaky breath. Sweat dots his brow as he peeks around me. "Now what?"

"We should probably move farther away in case any of them find the ceiling entry and pop their heads up to look for us."

He agrees, and I click on the flashlight, crawling on my hands and knees under the low roof until we make it next to the air conditioning unit. I edge around it until I'm safely hidden from sight, and he does the same.

"It's hot up here," he releases a breath, as more sweat droplets drip down his brow.

"There are roof fans around the dome. Otherwise, the only cool air is what escapes right here." I thumb toward the big machine and the leak in a huge tube leading off of it. The tube's been patched twice since I took over The Pit, but the air's so strong that the patches keep bursting. The tube needs to be replaced, but I can't afford it yet. "Switch me spots, so you're closer to it."

His head cocks to the side, his lips tucked into a thoughtful grin. I smile in return and his dusty palms land on my cheeks, pulling me to him. His kiss is sweeter this time rather than all-consuming. It's different than we've shared before like he's rewarding me for being thoughtful. His tongue tangles with mine before he draws away, taking my bottom lip with him. He sucks it in his mouth, making me groan with pleasure.

We switch spots, and he pulls me to sit next to him. "I'm sweaty, but I prefer you close."

My shoulders bounce in a shrug. "I don't mind you sweaty. You forget we've been naked and sweaty together."

"I could never forget," he mumbles, and it could be one of the sweetest things I've heard from him yet.

MERCENARY

Having her next to me, smelling her scent and mine mingled has my groin tightening and my cock growing heavy. I just fucked her not even an hour ago, but I can't seem to get enough of being inside her. Once I started last night, I couldn't seem to stop. We're both going on barely any sleep, and I can't think of a better reason to be up all night than being with her.

"What do we do now?" she whispers.

"We could make out," I mutter, and she laughs.

"I think we're way past that point already."

"Nah, you can never be."

She grins and my lips land on hers again, only this time my kiss is far more heated. Pushing her onto her back, I brace myself over her. The massively sized air conditioning blocks our bodies to keep us out of sight from the ceiling door. The cool air blows over both of our bodies in this position, rewarding us for our lust.

I take her mouth with a fervor closely matching the first time I wrapped her tightness around my cock in front of the clubhouse. Pushing her shirt up to bare her breasts, my mouth leaves hers to suck each of her nipples into my mouth. She's delicious with creamy skin that reminds me of silk. I could touch her for hours and never have my fill of her.

"Mmm..." She hums in her chest, the sound drawn out as her hips twist side to side. Her nipples are a direct link to her core. I learned that if you want to get Chevelle turned on immediately, go for her tits. She loves when I play with her pussy too, but her breasts are hypersensitive.

"You should pierce these succulent tits, with just a flick of my tongue, your panties would be drenched."

"They already are."

"Damn, I love it that your pussy gets so wet for me."

My tongue trails over her tummy, licking at the soft, smooth flesh, tasting a bit salty. It's hot up here, and we're both sweating. Rather than it turning me off, it does the opposite. I want to see her drip with it, all because my body drives her completely wild.

Her chewed-down fingernails rake through my spikey hair that's the color of freshly poured asphalt. Our features closely match, both of our flesh is dotted with a light tan. Her hair and mine are nearly the same — the only big difference is our irises; mine are like ice — blue, cold, and ruthless. Hers, on the other hand, are like embers — the light tawny color full of warmth and honey.

"Oh yes. God your mouth is perfect," she whimpers with desire. Her hips rise until she can create some type of friction for her pussy against my arousal.

My teeth clamp down, biting into the only fleshy part of her tummy. The move elicits another enticing moan from her. The sound makes me feral inside, wanting to rip her jeans away and take her with a force some would deem unsafe. She belongs to me, and with every breath, I want to mark her so deeply that another wouldn't dare attempt to take her from me.

Is this love? No. Not yet, anyhow. This is passion so fierce with each thrust, claiming another's body so desperately that when you do finally fall in love with them, it consumes your soul entirely.

When I give Chevelle all of me, she'll have the power to take my life if she desires. That's the amount of devotion she'll gain from me. At that point, I will no longer be able to survive without her. I'd simply cease to exist if I loved her as she deserves, without knowing she's enraptured the same way in return.

My fingers land on her pants button and in my haste, yank the material apart. The zipper protests but then relinquishes its hold as well. Chevelle's palms land on each of my cheeks, wrenching my head up to meet her fiery gaze. On a wispy breath, she demands, "Take me, Mercenary, please."

I'll take her all right. I'll fucking keep her too. My hands fly back on course, and I sit back on my haunches.

Stripping the tight jeans free from her, I toss them to the side. She's bare. In our hurry, she never stopped to put on panties, and at her exposed pink folds I groan with desire.

Leaning in, I plant my nose to her pussy and inhale deeply. She smells sweet with her need. The scent mingles with my come from earlier, and the knowledge has me wanting to roar in pleasure. She's pure sex, and it calls to everything inside me to slam my cock into her deep, to keep my scent on her.

"You're so goddamn enthralling," I murmur, tilting my head to lick up the inside of her thigh. "I knew you needed to be fucked when I first laid eyes on you. This pussy needed to be owned and now look at it, soaked for me."

She moans, and I in turn to do the same. My tongue caresses her other thigh, lapping at the wetness from her excited core. I want more. I want to bury myself in her and never come up for air.

"You want me to lick your wet pussy, sweetie, or you want me to fuck it?" I've never given her a decision before, but I'm feeling generous after she's taken my cock so wantonly all night.

"I want you inside," Chevelle admits. She meets my eyes as I trail my gaze from her pretty pink center to over her flat tummy. I take in every inch of her curvy hips and full, round breasts. She's utterly sensational. Her body's made for a man's pleasure—*for mine*.

"Mine," I let out a growl as my tongue trails upward again. It moves over her stomach, through the valley of her tits and stops with me tenderly biting her chin. My lips find hers soon after, a kiss overtaking her mouth as I line up the head of my dick to her blissful center.

She breaks away from my lips to heave in a deep breath and firmly proclaims, "Mine."

Her dainty hands grab my ass cheeks, yanking me to her, my cock impaling her pussy. Rather than scream at my huge size plunging inside her fully, she moans against my throat. Her little mouth finds my flesh with her teeth, biting as I adjust to go deeper and draw a whimper from her. She wants all of my length in her, even if it brings a touch of pain laced with the pleasure.

"You know my cock's big, sweetie. Why'd you hurt yourself with it?"

"Mmm," she hums, sucking my skin between her lips.

She releases me, and I move again as her tongue licks along my neck to draw my lobe into her mouth next. Her palms apply more pressure to my ass, and I grind against her in response. Breathily she orders, "I want to be fucked biker boy. I have so much adrenaline inside, I could tear you up right now. If I didn't have to be quiet, I'd scream the walls down right now with how badly my body craves yours. *Make me come.*"

"Careful with your words, little woman, or I'll be the one tearing this pussy up. I don't want to hurt you, but I will if you provoke me. I fuck to own, Chevy."

"Please?" she begs, moving her hips to create more friction between us and it's my undoing.

Grabbing her hands from my ass, I pin them both in one of mine above her head. My free hand wraps around her throat, holding her in place as I gain my bearings and start to pummel into her. She's frightened but doesn't want to admit it. I can feel it in my gut. She needs me to take the control from her. She craves this more than anything, to keep her distracted from the danger literally underneath us.

Her mouth falls open as near silent moans and whimpers escape her as I continue my assault. Mere moments pass before her cunt grips me like a vise, squeezing and pulling. The hungry muscles attempt to force the come from my cock with its needy little sucks. Her pussy wants me to claim it.

"You're mine, Chevelle."

Her mouth closes to swallow as her climax begins to fade away, and I squeeze her throat in my grasp, stealing the air from her. "Say it," I demand, never pausing in my assault. My nuts grow heavy, full of my seed wanting to mark her in ways others won't be able to see.

She gasps, and I squeeze tighter. I don't stop until her other hand pushes against my hand, as she attempts to break free. She fights with my fingers stealing her oxygen.

Thrusting into her hard, I offer an ultimatum. "You'll say it, or else I'll squeeze your fucking throat until you pass out." My dick expands, my come nearly about to burst as I take her as she desired but also demand her to admit my ownership. There's a price for her pleasure, my own pleasure.

"Yes," she mouths, and I briefly release my hold. My hand rubs against the bruised flesh in soft massaging circles to get the blood flowing again.

"What was that?" I order and again squeeze her sensitive flesh. This time my grips tighter than before, but only for a beat. I want to cut off her oxygen quick enough to immediately spike her adrenaline.

She throws her head back, a deep moan braking free as an even stronger orgasm overtakes her body. I move my hand, resting the palm in the middle of her breasts. Her eyes meet mine, and she breathes, mid climax, "I'm so fucking yours."

The way she proclaims the words makes them powerful. I roar out my own release. The come bursts from my tip, coating her insides with my dense essence. I brace over her until I'm fully spent. My face drips with sweat. It trails over my bare back and chest. My breaths come deep, as I try to regain my bearings.

Chevelle's so utterly divine right now—lying below me sated and thoroughly fucked after she's admitted to being mine. "Beautiful," I whisper. Her body flushes for an entirely different reason than the heat and spontaneous bought of sex.

She's like a flower. Soft and colorful with breathtaking beauty on the outside, full of thorns to protect herself with, and resilient on the inside, always seeking out the sources to keep her alive. She's strong, stubborn, and motivated. Those three on a woman make up such a magnificent creature.

And she's *mine*. I think that's the part that fills me the most. Being in her presence and knowing that I'm lucky enough to have her in my life. She could have chosen anyone and yet she's let me in. Not anybody else.

"Did I break you?" I mumble, and she giggles. Chevelle actually giggles, and I find myself wishing I could wrap the tinkling sound around me always. "And what is the sweet smell on your throat?"

"Oh, it's Calvin Klein Eternity Air for women."

How fitting, I think with a pleased grin. *Air*. It definitely suits her when I think of being without her—not being able to breathe properly. She's my own air.

"I like it."

"I'm glad," she replies and reaches for her shirt. I grab it before she can and shake out the dust, and then help work it over her head. "I can do it." She takes over.

"I know," I mutter, even though I didn't want her to. I was enjoying dressing her after undressing her. Rather than sulk like a child giving up his most precious belonging, I go about pulling my jeans over my ass and buckling them.

I was so consumed with her I don't recall even unbuttoning them or shoving them free from my cock. One minute we're sitting here, she's asking me to fuck her and then I was. That sums it up in my mind. Once her tits were bared, everything else just faded away.

She attempts to stand, but the ceiling's too low. When she starts to fall, losing her balance, I reach out, steadying her so she can finish getting her pants on. "Thanks."

"Of course. I'm the one that took them off, after all."

She grins about to respond when an even louder boom than before shakes the building.

Her eyes grow wide, her mouth dropping in surprise. "Shit! What was that?"

I shake my head. "I have no clue."

I'm a lying bastard too because I'm pretty sure that was another bomb and those fucks down there just blew something big up.

17. **Give me 6 hours to chop down a tree and I'll spend the first 4 sharpening the axe.**

- Abraham Lincoln

CHEVELLE

"They're ripping apart my race track. I have to get down there and stop them!"

He shakes his head, placing his hand on my arm. "There are too many, sweetie."

"I don't care if there are twenty of them. I can't afford to fix the damage they're inflicting on my home. I won't let them demolish what I've worked so hard for."

"I get it, but we have to wait, just a little longer."

I'm ready to argue my case more when sirens wail off in the distance. "Is that?" I gesture with my thumb toward the sound.

"Sounds like it," he agrees.

"Thank God. Never thought I'd be this excited to see the cops before." I release a breath and crawl toward the way we came in. Pressing my head against the thin panel, I try to listen for anything that'll clue me in on anyone nearby. After a few tense moments, I don't hear anything coming from the other side, so I lightly push the panel.

"Be careful," Mercenary scowls from behind me.

"I am," I mumble. Leaning my head out of the hole in the ceiling, I peer around the maintenance room. I pause a few more seconds to listen for talking or footsteps in the hallway. It's hard to concentrate with my heart beating so loudly in my chest; it feels like it could burst out at any moment. "All clear," I say, leaning back up.

"Let me lower myself first. You can jump down into my arms."

I agree, backing away a bit more. His thoughtfulness doesn't go unnoticed on my part. He's willing to jump down and risk his neck. He could easily let me go by myself, but he doesn't. Instead, he's going to catch me in his arms like some fairytale prince. I doubt princes wear leather and ride Harleys, but clearly, mine does.

226

He eases through the hole, dropping lithely like a ninja and holds his arms up for me, just as he'd offered. His muscles bulge from all the exertion he's putting on them, and it has me wanting to lick his biceps. "Ease your legs down first, babe. I'll be able to reach them and work your body down without you getting hurt."

He acts like I'm a china doll, but yet he forgets I flipped him flat on his ass the first time we met. Regardless, I find myself following his instructions, even though I don't need them. But for some reason, I want to please him, I want him to think I need his guidance, and that I value it. It's pretty damn sexy having a man that acts like a real fucking man doing man shit. He's nothing like these weak beta males floating all over the covers of magazines right now. I don't know what ever made them suddenly interesting, but I take pleasure in making those betas my bitches.

His thick arms wrap around my legs, carefully sliding me downward along his body. I'm breathing heavy when I come in line with his face and it's not from nerves. It's from his touch. He presses a tiny kiss to the tip of my nose and keeps lowering me until my feet hit the ugly scratched tile floor.

"Stay behind me." He pulls the tranquilizer gun from his back pocket and hands it to me. I'd completely forgotten about it in my rush and then with the sex. He yanks his Glock from his holster attached to his jeans, and opens the door a crack, peeking out into the hall.

The siren outside stops and then a shout comes from the lower level. I race around Mercenary, passing my office door and around the corner. It's reckless, but I have to see what the hell is going on below. Keeping my body pressed against the wall, I lean my head forward just a smidge until I can make out the men at the very bottom. There's a group in the center, all their weapons pointed toward a lone cop walking into the main area.

"Put your weapons down!" The officer shouts sternly, and before I can blink, a random gun discharges a bullet. It slams into the cop, and he immediately hits the ground.

I utter a whispered, "Fuck," just as Mercenary steps beside me.

"What is it?" he murmurs quietly.

"They just shot a freaking cop! He's on the ground."

"Fuck, this is bad."

"Surely there are more police with him?"

He shrugs. "Not if it was one that's in Viking's pocket. He could've been closer than the guys and stopped in to be a distraction."

"Damn it. More like a dead distraction, the poor guy. What if he has a family?"

"Viking will help take care of them; he'd never leave them on their own."

A roar combined of various engines comes from outside, the sound echoing in the dome shaped building.

"Hopefully that's our backup and not theirs."

I nod, holding my breath as moments after the engines quiet, a few bikers edge their way inside, weapons drawn. The guys below automatically begin popping off bullets like it's the goddamn Wild West and the Oath Keepers all dodge in several directions to take cover behind rows of seats. They exchange fire as another group of Oath Keepers silently enter The Pit from the back entrance we use for deliveries.

I watch with rapt fascination. The drama below unfolds so quickly right before my eyes. I can't seem to look away no matter the danger.

The door down the hall next to my apartment creaks opens, and Mercenary pokes his head back around the corner, Glock ready to shoot. He relaxes his gun filled hand, pointing it toward the floor to click the safety in place and leans back next to me with a deep exhale.

"What was it?"

"It's Odin. I texted him when I pushed you up in the ceiling again, so he'd know where we were. I didn't want to take them by surprise and have a brother shoot us by mistake."

So that's what had taken him so long to get in the ceiling with me, besides searching out the flashlight.

As soon as he's finished filling me in, Odin's head appears around the corner. "You both okay?" he asks, and we nod, our faces quickly turning to watch the scene unfold below.

"Give me the tranq gun." He holds his hand out to me.

"What, why?" I place it in his palm.

"I'm going to see if I can help my brothers and keep a few of these fuckers alive to torture later."

I draw in a harsh breath, knowing how true his words are. I know they won't hesitate to hurt the rival biker club members, but I prefer to pretend to be ignorant to it all. Odin and I watch as Mercenary picks off two more guys before a few turn their heads up, looking for us. It's enough of a distraction that the Oath Keepers have time to riddle the remaining threats with bullets.

With the cease of weapons, we're drenched in silence. It's so stark, it's nearly louder than the shooting was, it seems. My shoulders drop, the muscles in my back starting to unwind from the tightness leaving my body, knowing we're finally safe. I'm going to be sore from being strung so damn tight during this whole thing rather than from fighting.

A loud boom rattles everything in the building pulling a harsh curse from me. Mercenary yanks me to his chest, his arms wrapped around me tightly to protect me. Holding onto the railing beside us, I lean over to see a few Oath Keepers had fallen with the blast, but no one looks injured from it.

"We need to get down there."

"The fuck was that?" Odin sputters. His mouth's slack with shock from the explosion.

"Bombs," Mercenary grits. "The motherfuckers have set off three since they showed up.

"Holy shit," he curses, and we both nod our agreement. "We found the guys out front that you knocked out earlier."

"Good." Mercenary reloads the tranquilizer gun and hands it back over to me. I grip it tightly, afraid I may accidently shoot someone and knock them out. I don't say it aloud, but the thought does bother me. He grabs my hand as we head for the stairs to join the others.

Odin keeps talking as we travel down the steps in a rush that lead to the delivery hall and back entry to The Pit. They take a few stairs two at a time, but my legs are too short, and I nearly have to jog to keep pace. "Torch has them tied up and waiting in the back of the truck."

"A cop showed up; he was shot dead upon entry."

I listen idly, concentrating on not falling and busting my ass. With one hand firmly planted to the banister, the other remains secure in Mercenary's firm grip.

"Son of a bitch. This is going to be a big fucking mess."

"Prez here?"

"Yeah, he's down there." Odin doesn't even sound winded. What the hell do these guys do to stay in such good shape? Yeah, I can fight, but shit, it's not like I do cardio or anything.

On the next break between levels, I run my hand through my dusty hair. Using the band around my wrist, I twist my long locks up into a topknot. This seriousness definitely calls for it.

"You okay, Chevelle?" Mercenary flicks his gaze over me as we make our way down the next flight of stairs and my hand shoots out to keep my balance.

"Honestly, I have no idea how to answer that," I mutter, thinking over the carnage I just witnessed in the middle of my beloved race track. He gives my hand a squeeze, and both of them stay quiet after that until we make it to the main level.

"Is it clear?" Odin calls out and gets a few yesses in return.

We enter in the middle of a heated debate. Nightmare scowls, his voice raised as he drills in his point. "We need to hit these fuckers now! Enough waiting. They were here to kill more of ours, and with a big hit like this, they won't be able to react to us right now."

"We have to wait, brother," Viking argues. His right hand tugs at his beard in frustration.

Nightmare flings his arms out. "Fuck waiting! I've been patient enough, we attack now."

Odin interrupts, "And walk into the unknown? They could end up killing us all."

Nightmare shakes his head, exasperated. "Man the fuck up, O. You're the new VP. Time to see just how savage you are, brother." He lays down the challenge, but rather than jumping on it, Odin just shakes his head.

"If it was the right move, I'd be all for it, but it's not. We've left them alone for this long, and it's throwing them off. We've been patient and have just picked off...how many?" He glances around, his fingers moving as he counts the bodies littering the floor. "Fifteen, at least?"

Viking agrees, confirming the count at sixteen Iron Fists total. The thought of killing sixteen people, even if they were evil, makes me feel sick to my stomach.

Odin carries on. "That's blowback we've inflicted on them without them even being aware it was us doing it. They may suspect, but they have no way of proving it. Unless they were to all just show up right now or have spies in place."

He glances at his fellow club members and then looks back to Nightmare, continuing. "You telling me that you can pull the same off by showing up at one of their clubs to get retaliation? You may cut the snake, but it won't be the head brother. I don't know about everyone else, but if we're going after a snake, I want it dead. I'd rather plan to cut the entire fucking head off and not worry about it coming back around to sink its teeth into me."

Brothers around the room murmur their agreement, and Viking gazes at his younger sibling, more like a proud poppa than a blood brother. "He's right, Night." The Prez agrees.

Mercenary cuts in. "What are we going to do with all these bodies? Anyone can walk in right now. I'm sure the first fucking bomb was them blowing a hole in the entry."

Viking grunts. "You're right, a big fucking hole's there." He glances at me, empathy in his gaze. He knows this place is my life. "O and Torch look for something to block the front from curious visitors. See if you can find some plywood or similar for the time being."

They both stride off toward the front and Viking continues barking orders. "Saint and Sinner, make sure they're all dead in here and anyone still breathing, tie them up." He holds out some thick zip ties. The guys snatch them and take off to do as ordered.

"Nightmare, back the pickup to the loading bay door. We'll get these bodies loaded that way." He turns to an older man. "Smokey check supplies for the largest black trash bags you can find. We need something to wrap these bodies in. Oh, and some duct tape."

"You got it, boss," the old timer rasps.

"Mercenary, take your woman to her apartment to gather whatever belongings she needs. No more bullshitting around. She stays at the club until this is sorted. I knew I should've sent someone out here last night to get you guys to come back."

I don't have anything in me to fight him about it right now. My mind and body are still in shock over what just transpired here. Part of me is glad they're here. Obviously, they have a better idea of what to do to take care of everything. I wouldn't have a clue where to begin.

He gestures toward the back entry. "Chaos, start carrying the dead bodies to the bay door. They need to be wrapped and loaded. I'm going to find some mops and bleach buckets to get this shit show of evidence cleaned up."

I listen to Viking still barking off orders as Mercenary leads me back to the stairs, ears still ringing from the blasts.

18. Here's to chasing your dreams in the cutest pair of shoes you own.
- BossBabe

MERCENARY

Now that I'm coming off of the spike in my adrenaline, thinking there was a chance I wouldn't be able to protect Chevelle in a room full of that many men, I'm livid. She never should've been put in that position in the first place. Who the fuck do these jokers think they are, coming heavy at her like that? She's one fucking woman for heaven's sake!

I see the Prez's point, not wanting to attack right this minute to retaliate. At the same time, I'm with Nightmare. I never want Chevelle to be frightened again. She may have put up a brave front, but I felt her trembling next to me on those stairs when we watched those filthy dicks shoot the cop. I know she thinks she's strong, and to a point she is, but this is too much for her. She's a rough woman, trying to make a good life for herself, and if it wasn't for these fuckers, she'd be doing just that.

Her hold on my ribs loosens as I pull my Harley to a stop at the compound. Dropping the kickstand, I swing my leg over my seat and then grip her waist to help her off too. She's more than able to do it on her own, but I can't stop myself from touching her. Placing my arm over her shoulder, I tuck her into my larger frame, and we walk together inside. "You okay, sweetie?"

She sighs, her dark hair floating out of her face as the air conditioner hits us crossing the threshold. "There's no way I can fix the track in time for Saturday, and I have to race. I don't like leaving my cars there without me, either."

"No, you don't. Besides, it's not safe right now. As for your cars, I already told you, the brothers will bring them here for you."

Golden embers burn in her irises as they meet mine. She's wound tight, ready to argue with me. "Yes, I do. I told you that's how I pay the mortgage for The Pit. I can't afford to miss a chance to win, but I also don't have the cash for what it'll take to fix everything in time. I'm screwed."

Releasing her, she turns her body my direction. My hand reaches up, and my thumb trails over her bottom lip then along the curve of her jaw. She's upset, and I don't know what to do with a woman who's melancholy. Pissed off, yes...turned on, yes...hungry, yes...but not like this.

"I'll fix it," I promise before thinking it through.

"Thank you, cupcake, but you're already letting me take over your space and time to help keep me safe."

I shrug. "It's no big deal."

When my hand drops away, she leans forward, placing a tender, chaste kiss on my mouth. It's so insignificant that it means way more than any touch she's shown me since we've met. It's tender. Nothing is coaxed or heated about it. It's full of real feelings.

"It is to me. Not many men come around who give a shit; they all want something in return."

"I'll fix it," I repeat. This time I know exactly what I'm saying, and I mean it one hundred percent.

She offers a sweet smile, so non-Chevelle like. I think the craziness has her a bit shaken up. Whatever it is, I have to keep my guard up because kisses and smiles like those will have a man falling all over his own two feet. They're the type that'll have a man planning his future out.

We're interrupted by Blaze. He's back behind the bar, polishing the top until each bit shines. "Merc, everyone okay?"

"Hey, brother. Yes, they made it through okay."

"Thank God." He releases a heavy breath, and I tug Chevelle with me to sit on the stools in front of him.

"You here with Princess?" He's Vikings cousin and the Prez's ol' lady's personal guard. After the stories I've heard about what she's gone through, can't say I blame him for putting a steady man with her all the time.

"Yeah, you know with their past, Viking told her what was going down. Prez doesn't keep anything from her anymore to keep her safe. Anyhow, she gets worried about shit like this and she starts cooking like crazy."

"Cooking?" I cock an eyebrow as he gestures to his beer. Chevelle and I both nod, wanting a cold drink.

He grabs two longnecks, pops the tops and places them in front of us on coasters. "The first time shit went down with her, she'd been making a bunch of food to welcome the brothers home off a run. She and Vike were barely fucking back then. Anyhow, shit hit the fan, and it's been a way to ease her anxiety since then."

"Hard to imagine P having any sort of anxiety."

He nods. "She does and pretty badly when shit like this goes down. Probably a bit of PTSD mixed in with it too. She's really good at bluffing. We better drop it. If Viking catches any of this convo, we'll be missing skin for it."

With a chuckle, I throw back a hefty gulp. "You hungry, Chevy?"

"I could go help," she offers.

"You don't cook," I reply, puzzled.

Blaze smiles at her warmly. "Go on back there, darlin'. Princess will be happy for the company. Take your beer, and I'll fix a pitcher of frozen Margaritas."

"Margaritas?"

He nods, his smile growing. "Yeah, trust me, it's a P thing."

I press a kiss to her temple and point in the direction of the kitchen.

"She ever meet Princess before?" He turns back to me.

"I don't think so unless Viking took her to The Pit or something. You sure she won't care about Chevelle going back there?"

He shakes his head, refilling the plastic square container off to the right of me with a stack of bar napkins. "No, she needs the distraction."

"It doesn't piss the Prez off that you know his ol' lady so well?"

His gaze grows weary; he rakes his hand over his face. "In that first attack when I met her, I nearly killed her."

My eyes grow wide. That was definitely not what I was expecting from him. I know he was part of the group that came for Viking and Princess was attacked, but everyone left out the part of Blaze being one of the attackers. "Fuck."

He blows out another breath, busying his hands further by filling a container with straws. "I'll do whatever I can to make her happy and keep her safe. She's become a little sister to me, and the thoughts of what I was planning to do to her will haunt me for the rest of my life. If making her pitchers of margaritas, helping her cook, and keeping her safe makes her forgive me in some small way, well then it's all worth it."

"I get it. I'm trying to keep Chevelle safe too, but these dicks just won't stop."

"That's the Iron Fists for you. Those motherfuckers nearly killed me. I can't wait until the club snuffs the life from every single one of them."

"They trashed The Pit. I need to figure out how to fix it for her. She can't afford to hire anyone, and I don't want her there in case they show back up and try killing her again."

"What exactly needs to be done?"

"Mostly asphalt and concrete work, I think. The main entry has to be redone too." I finish off my beer while he blends the tequila mixture.

He pours the frozen strawberry tequila concoction into a plastic pitcher and grabs a few of the colorful plastic cups we've used in the past for barbecues. "Odin has an in with the

City," he mentions, moving around the bar to grab everything he needs. "He may know someone who can help with the asphalt. Torch knows how to pour concrete. I think Nightmare might, too. If you give them a hand, I'm sure they wouldn't mind helping you."

"No shit? Appreciate it, Blaze."

He taps the bar top with one of the plastic cups. "Bartending isn't just making drinks...you hear everything. You ever want to learn about the brothers around here, jump back behind the bar and mix shit up for a night."

"I'll stick to racing and motorcycles." I shrug, and he nods, heading for the kitchen.

A week passes quicker than I'd like it to. A few of the brothers and I have been keeping busy at The Pit. Blaze was right about Odin knowing someone with the City. Turns out it's the manager who owed Odin a favor. My brother called it in, and one evening a handful of workers showed up to patch the asphalt that one of the bombs had blown to shit.

Torch knew how to pour concrete like it'd been his profession in another life. Nightmare helped, grumbling the entire time that it'd get one more thing out of the way, so he could have his revenge. Saint showed up one day with an old gate. He'd found it out at the pig farm by the compound. Viking welded some hinges on it, and a brother named Spin from the other charter sanded the metal and painted it. Once we repaired the concrete up front, we turned the gate sideways, so it was long enough to cover the open space and secured it. Chevelle now has a steel barrier to help keep unsavory folks from breaking in the front entry.

Over the week together, Chevelle and I fell into an easy routine. It was like she was an extension of myself. She has no clue about anything we've done to fix up The Pit. I got ahold of Ace, and he's been handling everything as far as the races and business deliveries go. I've led Chevelle to believe we've been watching her business, but it's too dangerous for her to be there right now. Surprisingly, she's listened, and I'm guessing her seeing the Fists in action up close has put the severity of the situation in better perspective for her.

I think the only thing that's kept her sane through the time away is that we brought her cars to the compound with us. She's had full use of Viking's garage and the tools he has in there is no joke. It's a mechanic's wet dream and Chevelle has been tinkering with her own vehicles and any other that's been near the garage. It's kept her busy and distracted enough not to notice my lack of presence.

The nights, however, I walk in filthy, covered in sweat, while she treks in full of grease. It's hotter than hell seeing her all dirtied up from working on vehicles. We shower, and she lets me wash her body until every speck is clean. In return, she does the same for me, and it's become my favorite part of the day.

Being around her like this is almost too easy, and it's a bit disconcerting. Of course, I want a woman. Every man with half a brain wants one, especially a female like Chevelle. Doesn't mean I was expecting to start imagining her on the back of my bike every day or keeping her things here or staying with her permanently at The Pit. When I came across her lithe body the first day, those thoughts were the furthest from my mind. I wanted to fuck her, to make that smartass mouth of hers scream my name while I made her climax. Now I'm finding out that I don't want to stop.

"Ready, sweetie?" I grumble watching her pull on her jeans. They're so tight the damn things mold to every curve from the waist down. She needs a pair with my name across the ass so fuckers won't stare.

I'm doing a man pout thing right now because she told me we have to eat food before I can be inside her again. I offered to grab the peanut butter, but she said no. My babe wants tacos so, of course, she's getting them. Little does she know we're actually going to The Pit. It's Saturday. We've fixed everything, and the brothers have done a full sweep of the property.

I don't have to worry about her cars because they've been parked at the club under our watch. She's been so busy spending time under their hoods that I know she has them all race ready, just waiting for the chance. I feel like a fucking chick, excited inside because she's going to get to race, and rather than being a bitch or pain in the ass thinking she wasn't going to, she's taken it in stride. I can't wait to see her face when she realizes what's happening tonight. Not only that, but Ace has rounded up three sets of racers tonight. The Pit will make more money than it usually does on an average weekend.

"The weather's starting to change; it'll be a nice night on your bike." She smiles at me in the parking lot, and I lean in to kiss her.

"Which is your favorite car?"

She snorts. "Please cupcake, you don't ask a girl that sort of thing."

Jesus, I love this woman and the way she thinks—she's so different.

"Okay fine," I throw my hands up wearing a grin. "Not favorite, but if you had to pick one just for tonight, which would it be?"

She turns, gazing at her classic beasts all parked in a row. They're nice and shiny from the fresh washes she's given them the past two days. "I'm going with the Chevelle."

I grunt.

"Not because of why you'd think." She backtracks, and I stride toward the vehicle in question.

"Then why?"

She follows. "Not because it's my name, either. Although that's one of the reasons, it's always been my favorite."

"You're such a girl," I mutter, and she laughs.

"Not because she's the fastest..." She trails off, and I spin around, pulling her into me.

"So, tell me why."

"Because of the hood." Her face flushes and my gaze flicks to the hood. I was so far gone with her that night, furious at her for racing and also the guy hitting her and then burying my cock in her for the first time. The car escaped my mind.

"This is the car?" I stare at her, catching the way her breathing comes in little pants, her flushed skin and how her breasts suddenly seem too heavy for the bra she has on.

She rolls her eyes and copies me. "You're such a man."

With a cocky smirk, I yank her into my body, my cock ready for action. "A fact you can't deny." I take her mouth with mine again, this time turning her and laying her on the hood as my tongue makes love to hers. Her stomach grumbling breaks the spell, and I pull away, leaving her breathless.

"You're hungry babe, and I'm going to drive your favorite car."

"We're not taking the bike?" she asks after gazing at me for a few beats.

"No, you've been a good sport about riding it all week; we can take this pretty lady." I stroke the smooth, buffed paint. She no doubt waxed it this morning when I took off. It doesn't have any small flecks of dust like the others.

"I'll drive."

"Nope."

You know that saying you catch more bees with honey? The alpha in me hasn't quite figured that out yet, and I still find myself arguing and barking orders like she's a submissive.

"It's my car," she hisses.

Swallowing my pride to get her to let me drive so I can surprise her by going to The Pit, I momentarily tuck away the bossy attitude. "Please, sweetie? I haven't driven this one yet." I trail my fingers along the column of her neck, attempting to distract her from kicking my ass. I need to learn to just open up with words like this rather than demands. But she likes my bossiness in some shit, I can tell.

"Ugh," she groans. "Fine. But once you drive her, that's it. You're not keeping her, and I drive after that."

I chuckle. "Sure slugger. If that's what it takes right now to get you to give up the keys, I'll agree. Not saying I'll agree in the future, but one day at a time."

She rolls her eyes, her lips breaking out into an amused grin. "So charming." She tosses me her keys. It's a plain silver ring with a key for each vehicle.

"Hey," I point in her direction, rounding the car to the driver side. "You're welcome," I reply sarcastically with a pleased smirk.

"Oh lord," she sighs and climbs in to the passenger seat.

"That's what you were calling me earlier." I snicker with a wink and crank the engine.

19. Date a car guy.

We break parts not hearts.

CHEVELLE

Mercenary flies by the turnoff for the Taco Shack. I think nothing of it, writing it off as him joy riding in my Chevelle. Down the road a ways, he pulls my baby into The Pit and circles around the building to the back by the loading bay.

"What's going on?" I ask, shooting my gaze around. "Why are there cars here? I thought you told Ace to make sure everyone knew not to come in." The last thing we need are people in the building when they could get hurt, or worse, killed.

"They're here working," he replies absently, busily texting someone with one hand.

"You fixed the front? There wasn't any plywood or anything when we passed it. Was that a gate I saw at the entry?"

What have they been doing since I've been away? I thought they were just here to make sure no one tried to break in or blow up the place more than it already had been. I didn't know they were fixing anything. That's surprisingly thoughtful on the bikers' part.

He nods. "Yeah, we had to repair it, so no one would try breaking in."

Well, that makes sense. I'm still pleased to see it. It was hard enough leaving this place to begin with. I'm grateful for The Oath Keepers providing me with their protection, but The Pit is not only my business. It's my home as well.

"These people need to go home. The Pit won't make any money tonight to pay them to be here." And I won't be able to afford to pay for this place if I have employees around and no income coming in.

He shrugs. "We can talk about it inside."

I reach for the door handle, but when his palm lands on my other arm, I pause. Flicking my gaze back to him, he shakes his head.

"Wait." He tilts his chin toward the bay, and it rolls open.

I sit back as the bay door raises and Mercenary pulls in through the race and delivery entry. "At least no one's bothered with the back doors. I have to find something in this mess to be positive about."

"Relax, Chevy. We've had plenty of people here night and day to keep the Iron Fists away."

"It didn't stop them from setting up a car bomb the last time though," I mutter. My stomach squeezes at the not so distant memory. I've had a few random dreams about it all, and with each one, I've awakened covered in sweat. Thankfully Mercenary has been out like a light and hasn't witnessed me being a scared fruitcake in the middle of the night.

"They did that shit when no one was paying attention. Your employees know what to look out for."

"Oh yeah?"

He clears his throat and nods. "Odin filled them all in. Each one has my number to text if something's suspicious."

"They should be messaging me," I grumble as we drive past Sinner.

I wave, watching his dark gaze sparkle with amusement. He's been around a few times this week when I've argued with Mercenary over something random. The brothers find it highly entertaining to see me give cupcake shit as well as he dishes back to me. He'll learn eventually, though, that I'm not some meek woman. I'll stand up to him again and again until it sinks in. No man will ever push me around unless I ask him to.

The main door off the hallway is spread wide open, so we can drive right through. Usually, I keep it locked unless cars are loading and unloading to race. I don't like anyone snooping around the entry hall since the stairway off it leads to my apartment and office. You can never be too careful when it comes to creepers—especially now, I'm learning.

As soon as we get inside The Pit, Mercenary takes off, hauling ass around the track. Normally I'd be all for it, but the other club set off bombs and blew the track up along with various seating areas with a second bomb. His safety and mine, has me shouting to warn him, "What are you doing? We'll wreck!"

He shoots a confident smile at me and twists the volume to the radio up. He completely ignores me while we sail around the room in my favorite muscle car. This is the first time I've ridden with him driving a vehicle that's not a motorcycle; it reminds me a lot of myself. He's relaxed and appears to be completely in control. I swear if he wrecks my car, he'll never see that motorcycle of his again. I'll have it in a chop shop before he can blink and say *Chevy*.

The destroyed area comes into view and my stomach twists with nerves—my chest tightening until it feels like I can barely squeeze out a breath. If he doesn't slow down, we're going to crash and most likely roll. "Stop being reckless!" I yell over the stereo, nearly panicking as I scowl at him like he's nuts.

Swallowing roughly, it takes me a moment to realize we've actually passed the area completely. I try to spin around and get a decent look, to make sure I'm not losing my mind, but he's going way too fast, and we've sped right by it all while I was distracted trying to warn him.

With a deep breath, I sit back and attempt to coax my muscles into relaxing once again. Mercenary acts like this is just another day in the park, so maybe they laid concrete down or something. Watching everything as we speed over the track, he finally begins to slow down and eventually comes to a stop.

I nearly jump from the car before he shifts into park. Curious, I spin in a circle, searching for the damage caused by the rival bikers. It's completely gone. The place even appears better than it had when I initially bought it. The only way to tell something happened in this area is the lighter gray from the renewed concrete and the darker shade of black on the freshly paved road. It even smells of chemical cleaners and asphalt, another clue pointing toward the work that's been completed recently.

"No way," I comment to myself as I stand there staring, taking it in. A car door closes behind me, and Mercenary comes to stand beside me. On a whisper, I ask, "You did this?" My eyes flick to his.

With a small smile, he nods. "With help from everyone."

"I didn't know."

"I wanted to surprise you," he admits, and I swallow thickly at the gesture.

His thoughtfulness has me choking on emotions I'm not used to feeling. "I can't believe you did this. I will pay you back. I promise. Every single cent." And I will. It may take me five years, but I always settle my debts. I don't like owing anyone anything.

He grunts. "That's not what this is about."

"No?" I swallow roughly again with my voice higher and water swimming in my eyes. I need to keep these emotions locked up. I don't want him witnessing me so vulnerable. He's used to seeing me strong and capable, the way I prefer.

His finger tilts my chin up, gazing at me full of tenderness as I lick my lips. "Are you happy?" he asks, and it's said softly, not like the Mercenary I've grown used to full of rough edges and grouchy tendencies.

"So much," I admit with a grateful smile.

He beams, his bright white teeth on display, making me want to mimic him. "Well then, it was all worth it."

I can't hold back from leaping at him. He turns me all upside down with myself. It's like my body doesn't know what's up or down when it's near him and then he goes off and does something so kind and thoughtful like this making it even harder not to be sucked in even further with him. My arms wrap around his neck, and my lips find his. With a searing kiss, I attempt to show him just how much his actions really do mean to me.

The kindness reminds me of when I was younger and met the old man who stepped up to help me. It takes a special kind of guy to care for someone like that. Breaking away, I rain kisses all over his cheeks and chin. "Thank you."

He chuckles, setting me back on my feet. The man is as tall as a mountain. "You're welcome."

"I mean it; I'll pay you back."

"Don't worry about it. The guy who repaved that portion of the track owed Odin a favor. And Torch knew how to lay concrete and form up everything for the stairs. With everyone else helping as well, the only thing I came out of pocket for was the concrete." He shrugs, waving it off.

"Then the concrete—"

He interrupts. "No. You lent me your car to race in the beginning without batting an eye. If it wasn't for that, I wouldn't have been able to even win a race here. You helped put that cheddar in my pocket. Not that it would matter; I did this because I wanted you to be pleased, not so you'd pay me back."

Biting my lip, I go up on my toes to kiss him again. He's a giant dick, but when it comes to me, he's a big softy. Who'd have thought? "That explains everyone here too." I gesture around, taking in the employees carrying out various tasks.

He smirks, pulling my bottom lip in between his. Releasing it, he rasps, "No, sweetie. Everyone's here because Ace set up three races tonight, and you've got the first run. We've got plenty of Oath Keepers around to help with security as well so you can enjoy yourself tonight."

I'm stunned. The man has made me speechless with the degree of his thoughtfulness. Did he...plan this? Not only is the front fixed, but the track and the seating too, and he did it all without me having the slightest clue about any of it. I never would've thought *sweet* would be an appropriate word for him, but that's exactly what he's being.

"You all right?" he questions after a beat.

"We need to go to my place." And right the fuck now.

"I thought you were hungry. Tacos, remember?"

"Oh, I am, cupcake, but my hunger's for something else entirely." I don't think I've ever wanted to jump a man so damn badly as I do now.

"Yeah?"

I nod. "I'm thinking eight inches long, and three inches wide will fill me up quite perfectly."

"It sure the fuck will," Mercenary agrees, yanking me against his body.

In the next breath, he's trekking across the track toward the hallway, carrying me right along. My legs wrap securely around his waist and my arms around his neck to hold on while he strides like a man possessed. Leaning in closer, I draw his lobe between my teeth, applying enough pressure to make his chest rumble with need. I should've given him one hell of a blow job before we left. He definitely deserved it. Instead, he was thinking of what would make me happy again. I wanted food to eat, and he didn't even blink at my request. Then he brought me here to surprise me and fill me with even more good news.

What kind of a man puts a woman's happiness before his own?

A good one.

20.

MERCENARY

We eventually make it to her apartment upstairs after what feels like takes forever. I'll say one thing: those fucking steps suck. They're almost enough to put a damper on my aching cock, but I'm not one to skimp on a decent workout, so I decide to consider it my warm-up. I can fuck all night—what's a few stairs thrown in, carrying a woman up the entire way? With how she's been kissing and sucking on my neck, I'd almost consider the trek foreplay at this point.

"I can't believe you did all this," she says again, regarding me as if I've hung the moon. I'm used to attitude from Chevelle—hostility, even heat—but this wanton, tender gaze she's shooting me now is something entirely new.

"I had help, it wasn't all me."

"But it's you who came up with this…don't attempt to deny it. Admit it. You have a soft spot for me, cupcake." She smirks, and I grumble to myself something not making much sense, cause she's so fucking cute all happy and turned on.

Rather than egging her further, I pull her shorts and undies free then sit on the edge of the bed. I push her over to the side and position her so that her ass is up, front and center on my lap. The rest of her hangs to the side, her hands on the floor and her head hanging. I have her just where I want her. Flushed and ready for me has her looking beyond stunning.

"So fucking sexy," I mumble, holding her in place with one hand. My fingers on my free hand trail through her slit, relishing in the wetness. "You're so ready, sweetie…fucking drenched. You're craving my cock, huh?"

"Yes," she confesses. "Are you going to let me up, so I can have it?"

"Not yet. I will when I'm ready."

"So bossy."

I shrug, but she can't see me. Not that it matters, because it's true. I am bossy, and I don't care in the slightest bit either. "Mmm…but would I be bossy still if I was to sink my fingers into this pretty pink wet hole and make you feel good?"

"Maybe not quite as bossy, then," she replies, her tone heavy with her pent-up desire.

One digit trails through her slit and I draw in a breath with anticipation. The wait is always the hardest. I want to bury myself in her and never come up for air. So far, she's been pretty good with me taking her body when I want it. The first few times she made me work for it, but now all I have to do is stroke her the right way, and she's damn near purring with need for my cock.

I wonder how she'd feel if I really did keep her? She may be my ol' lady in the club's eyes, but we haven't established anything else between us as far as our relationship goes. I should do that before she has a chance to slip through my fingers. I have a feeling if she were to walk out of my life right now that I'd survive, but I'd damn sure miss her, and that's something I don't want to experience.

"Tell me, Chevelle," I murmur, petting her pussy without pausing. "What do you think this is between us?"

The muscles in her thighs tense, along with her back but she doesn't tell me to stop touching her. "Aren't I your ol' lady?" Her voice is small, almost unsure. My Chevelle has really let her guard down with me today, and I couldn't be any more pleased with it.

"You are, but do you know what that really means?"

"I have a good idea." She releases a breath as I push a finger into her heat.

"You're my property. You belong to me, and I always take care of what's mine."

"I'm no one's property; I've already told you this." She huffs as I draw my finger free.

Rather than inserting it again, I cup my hand and smack her drenched core. The wetness rolls down her thighs, and fuck me, every bit of me wants to bend over and lick it all clean.

"Wrong answer. That mouth is what got you in this situation in the first place. Had you been quiet, I'd have left you alone. Instead, you popped off, and I had to claim you to show you who's alpha. You craved my cock, and you got every fucking inch of it. Now, I get you in return."

She snorts, and I smack her pussy again. The air hits her in the right places but with my hand cupped, she gets no real contact, only the skin surrounding her core. It must be so frustrating to seek your pleasure and have it right there yet not be able to reach out and take it. Now she knows how I feel when it comes to her giving in to being my property.

"You can argue with me all you want, but it's the truth. You're mine, and I'll fight back even harder, sweetie. I have the cock, Chevelle. Dick runs this house, not pussy."

She pants as I smack her core again but offer her no relief.

"You are such an asshole." She squirms in my lap, her thighs beginning to vibrate with more pent-up desire.

"Never claimed to be anything different." I straighten my palm and lightly slap her pussy—once, twice, three times in a row. A loud moan breaks free and then pain spikes up my leg as she bites into my calf. Even with the jeans, her sharp teeth clamp down hard enough to cause me to draw in a quick breath.

Her mouth releases and I use my arm in a curl motion to pull her ass closer to my face. "Fuck," I breathe, my breath blowing over her glistening folds. She's so fucking turned on and ready for me, it nearly possesses me with want. Leaning forward, I bury my tongue in her core, licking and sucking at her center until she finally breaks and comes over my tongue.

Licking my fill, I rasp, "So sweet, Chevelle. You're a goddamn peach, ripe and aching to be bitten. I want your come all over my tongue and my cock...I want you everywhere."

Her hand fumbles to hold onto me, as she wiggles to get to me. She's still breathing hard, but eventually, I let her crawl over my lap. With eyes wild, hair a mess and so utterly beautiful, I can't help but gaze at her.

"I love peaches," she confesses and then plants her lips to mine, sweeping me up in a blistering kiss. Once she's had her fill of her taste in my mouth, she climbs down off my thighs.

Gazing up at me, her fingers move to my waist, tugging and working on my belt. Easing her struggle, I stand and yank the leather free. She plucks the button and pulls the zipper down. My cock falls forward, heavy with length and girth, finally free from being tucked up against my stomach.

"You have the biggest cock I've ever seen, ever felt...ever sucked," Chevelle admits, and my chest puffs a bit at the immense compliment.

Her small hands take my shaft, one working up and down, while with her other she lightly scores her nails along the tender flesh. Eventually, she stops at my full nuts. She caresses them and then grazes her nails in a motion that has my gut tightening.

"Fuck!" I gasp, ready to surrender my body to her. "You're good at that." My gaze meets hers, and I see power reflecting in her irises. She's the type of woman to let me *think* that I have all of the control when in reality it's hers.

"I haven't even put your cock in my mouth yet." She licks her lips, and I groan. I'm a cocky fool to have teased her earlier; now it's her turn to return the sweet torment.

Pushing my length up, she holds it against my groin with one hand and continues her assault on my balls with her other. Leaning forward, she draws one in her mouth and then switches, sucking the other in as well, swirling her tongue as her nails continue to caress the opposite.

"Fuck a damn peach; you're a goddess, babe."

She lifts my heavy sac off to the side and her tongue trails just on the underside of them. The action has me searching for something to grab on to. The sensations are insane. No one—and I mean no one—out of the many women I've been with have licked me there. *Holy shit!*

She sits back and swirls her tongue around the tip of my head. "Beg me," she orders.

I nearly choke at her command. "W-what?" I stumble like a fucking schoolboy.

She runs her finger under my nuts in the same spot she'd been licking and swirls her tongue around the head again. Shit feels so good, I may black out if she keeps it up.

"I said…" She nips at the tip of my cock, and I nearly come right there. "Beg. Me."

"Put it in your mouth, please?"

"Hmm," she hums with a tease and repeats the previous action again.

Precum coats the top of my dick in anticipation, and if she's this good, I'll say anything she wants to hear. I may just end up blowing my load all over her face if she keeps toying with me, and I'd rather it be inside her somewhere.

She swipes the head, lapping at the precum and scores her nails under my sac. It's the breaking point for me. "Please baby, please, just put my cock in your mouth or pussy…somewhere. Let me sink into that tight, wet pussy again."

Her mouth closes over me, and it's like being touched by a sex god. The woman swirls her tongue over me repeatedly. One hand works the bottom of my shaft side to side, and her other hand continues to pull and caress my balls.

"Holy shit, Chevelle!" My labored breaths speed up. "If you don't stop, I don't think I can hold myself back from coming," I admit, nearly purring from the sensations in my cock. She's had my dick in her mouth all of two minutes, and I'm ready to explode.

She doesn't even hesitate at my words, so I grab two handfuls of her hair and sink down as far as she'll let me go. Each thrust has her gagging, her throat attempting to close around the head of my shaft. Tears trail over her cheeks, but I don't break my rhythm. There's no turning back now. The bitch wanted it, well, she's getting it.

This is her fault, teasing me to the point of bursting; it makes a man nearly uncontrollable. I'm no different. If anything, I have even less control. My testosterone spirals through me, telling me to own every crevice of her flesh with my essence. *She's mine.*

One last pump and I'm shooting off. With a mighty roar that echoes through the room, my come coats the back of her throat. My seed's thick and warm as she swallows everything I offer. She takes control yet offers me submission all at the same time, and it has me nearly falling to my knees to worship at her feet.

Eventually, my throbbing resides, and I release the beautiful woman waiting patiently on her knees. She sits back, licking her lips like the cat that got the cream. She's no doubt pleased with her performance. Hell, I am!

"Feeling better?" She hikes a brow.

I yank her to her feet and return her blistering kiss from earlier. There are no words to fully explain to her how I'm feeling at the moment. Overwhelmed would be one of them, sated, insatiable, hungry, yet full. There are so many conflicting thoughts running rampant in my mind to voice them properly.

"Mmm," she sighs in my mouth as we part. My lips follow the path of her jaw and down over her throat. I nip and suck, not having enough of her taste. "I should do that more often."

"I won't mind, I promise."

Her laugh's husky with our passion. "I'll keep that in mind. Now, should we see what we can find to eat?"

"I'm not done with you yet," I promise and yank her shirt free.

"But you just...you can get it back up that quickly?"

My gaze flicks down, and she follows my stare. My cock hasn't even budged. I may have just come, but you'd never be able to tell by looking at my length. I grab her around the ribs, under her tits and easily toss her onto the bed. Chevelle's face flushes with surprise, and I hop in after her.

21. **If you don't look back
at your car after you park it,
you own the wrong car.**

- Truth

CHURCH

Everyone's tense as we pile into church, claiming our usual seats. Viking sent a massive text calling us here immediately.

Blaze shuffles in behind Chaos, the brothers' hands loaded with various cups and two bottles, one of whiskey, another of moonshine. They sit and pass the cups to the sides, so everyone will have one. We all hurried rather than stopping for a drink like we normally do. I've only been here about four months now, but I'm quickly catching on to how things are run around here.

Nightmare lights a smoke and then puts his pack and zippo in the middle of the table. Various brothers reach for it. Smokey grabs it first, taking one, lighting it, and passing it on. Odin's busily filling his tumbler half full of moonshine when Viking slams the gavel down.

"I called you all here for a reason," the Prez grumbles, pulling us from the various distractions. "Torch was able to break one of the Iron Fists we collected from The Pit a couple of weeks back."

We're so silent, waiting with anticipation that you could hear a pin drop.

"We got a final location. I called up Ruger, and he was able to do a little recon. He confirmed the Fists' location."

Nightmare's fist lands on the table. "Fuck, finally! It's been three goddamn weeks since they blew up The Pit and I'm sick of fucking waiting."

Viking nods. "I know brother, I know."

Saint sits forward, eager. "What's the plan, Vike?"

He lifts his hands up, conveying we need to chill the fuck out so he can finish speaking. "That's exactly why I called you in here. We need to all agree on how we want to handle this. Their attacks were personal. Not only have they tormented the other charter, but they targeted you specifically, Night. You're ol' lady and your son, Maverick. They hurt my Cinderella, and you all know I will scalp a motherfucker that touches my ol' lady. I want blood, as I'm sure all of you do. Blaze, they nearly killed you. Hell, they did kill Scot and Bronx. I say we make every last one of those motherfuckers bleed."

Everyone nods their agreeance, and I speak up. "They targeted Chevelle too, for over a month now. She's my ol' lady, and I'll do whatever I can to make them hurt."

A few brothers cast surprised glances at me, but I see something only a few had offered me already—respect. Viking meets my gaze. "We can use all the help we can get."

I take a swallow of the moonshine one of the brothers passed to me and then nod. He sets a phone on the table drawing everyone's attention back to him. We're forbidden to bring phones in this room, so this'll be good, I'm sure.

"Spidey wants us to put him on speakerphone when we discuss what our plan is. He and Ruger have been working together on the recon of the Fists for us." He hits a button and puts it on speaker.

"Yeah?" Spider barks into the phone.

271

"Spidey," Viking speaks loudly. "We're making plans, brother."

"Bet, I've been thinking up scenarios since we last spoke on how to go about hitting all three of their clubs at once. I'm putting you guys on speaker as well. I have Exterminator beside me."

"All right, what do you have for us?"

"From the cameras Ruger's set up and Google satellites, I've been able to pick up fairly decent images of the buildings and the surrounding areas. When we hang up, I'll send you an encrypted email with photos. Open it in my room on the blue laptop. It's secure."

Viking gestures to Torch, and he nods in agreement. "All right, I'll have Torch go over it with me when we get out of Church."

"So, we have a few options, but I'll bring up the one I think will be the most successful. Oh, first of all, is Ares' charter going to help out?"

"As far as I know, they are," Viking mutters. I've learned that the Prez is decent friends with the Prez of the other charter about thirty minutes away. I've met the brothers from there on a few occasions. They seem like good guys.

"Perfect. So, the Fists have a smaller building that has around ten guys there at any given time. I'm certain this is where they keep the drugs they distribute. I think it would be smartest to have Ares clean up that mess when we hit the others. I'll hack into one of the military's drones and use that to take out the other building that houses their weapons. They keep another ten or fifteen guys at that one. I think these spots are more like warehouses that they always keep guarded."

We all stare at the phone, eyes wide after hearing Spider declare he can hack into military grade weapons. The brothers have told me the guy is smart, but damn, that's an entirely different level of genius.

He continues. "That'll leave the main club open for you. The property is surrounded by an electric chain-link fence as the first line of defense. Odin should use his contact at the City and get a dump truck. You can ram through the fence, and a handful of the brothers can safely ride in the back. I'd bring a van to help haul the guys back home or something. If you go with this option, you need to come heavily armed and prepare for a fight. Even taking out the twenty or twenty-five at the other buildings, it leaves behind a good twenty or so at the main club."

"Christ," Viking gripes. "That plan actually sounds doable, and we have a chance at minimum injuries or blowback on our members."

"Exactly," Spider agrees.

It all sounds a bit nuts to me, but it's one hell of a plan, that's for sure.

Nightmare huffs. "I'm having flashbacks of our Mexico trip. Anything inside that fence we need to worry about besides a group of pissed off cunts posed as an MC club?"

I have no idea what he's talking about, but it must've been bad by the ashen tone of his face.

Viking's mouth drops open, a look I'm not used to seeing from him. Ever. "Fuck, good point, Night."

Spider speaks up. "No, no, nothing like that. Ruger has been watching the grounds himself and has reported back that there are no animals."

"Pretty sure I can't run from another lion again," Nightmare mutters, and I draw in a quick breath between my teeth. Fucking shit, a lion? No wonder Chicago sent me down here. They obviously think I'm just as wild as these fuckers.

Viking shoots his gaze around the room, landing on each of us. "Anyone else have anything to say?"

Everyone remains quiet.

"Good, then let's vote and work out the fine details."

Odin cracks his knuckles and begins. "Everyone in favor of Spider's plan vote aye. Any nays, offer up an explanation after voting is complete so we can look at other options."

Each of us agrees, ending with Odin commenting "aye" as well. There's not much to discuss when a member of the NOMADS talks about blowing up an entire clubhouse with military grade weapons.

"It's settled then. We'll go with Spider's plan unless something comes up and then we'll improvise. Do not show mercy to any of them. They will all be armed and ready to kill. I suggest you do the same."

"When will we ride out?" Odin questions and then drinks from his tumbler of whiskey.

"Spider? How much time do you need?" The Prez holds his gavel as he asks.

"An hour, maybe two."

"I'll call Ares and we'll get organized," he informs us. "Prepare to ride in three days if nothing spooks the Iron Fists." At that, he slams the gavel down, officially dismissing us.

I think most of us are in shock as we leave the room quietly and head straight for the bar. I'd left Chevelle in my room, asleep. It's been over a month already since the MC tried blowing up The Pit. She's remained here with me each night.

We've fallen into our own routine of sorts. I usually help her during the day with things at The Pit, and as the evening approaches, we make our way back here. Every night I come in here like a man possessed and tell her she's mine. I think she's finally beginning to realize that I mean it, and in return, I'm falling for her a little more each day.

When this is all over with the Iron Fists, I can't help but hope she'll stay. I want her safe, but I want her with me even more. I'm selfish, no doubt. And most of all, I'm not ready to give her up. I meant it when I said I want to keep her.

CHEVELLE

"How was church?" I greet the distracted biker as he enters our room. It was only his before all this began, but I've been staying here long enough to claim at least a quarter, if not half of it, as mine.

"Surprisingly productive." His mouth hikes up into a sexy grin.

"Nice. Anything about The Pit yet?"

His eyebrow skyrockets. He's already warned me about how he can't share any biker business with me. "No. But, if all goes right, you'll have less to worry about."

I'm surprised he's admitted as much so easily. I was expecting him to tell me to mind my own business. "So, you'll finally have me out of your hair, then."

His grin falls, his forehead wrinkling as his brows furrow. "Uh, no."

"No?"

He steps closer, pulling me to stand on the bed, so we're nearly the same height. The man is a freaking tower. I rest my palms on his wide, sturdy shoulders and his hands come to grip my waist. "You think once this is all over with, I'll up and pop smoke?"

I shrug, my throat growing tight. When did I catch a case of the feelings for this brute?

"Not happenin', sweetie. I'll still be there every Saturday night, racing your Camaro and taking home my winnings. Perhaps one day you'll even get the nerve to race me."

The snort escapes before I can smother it down. "You won't win."

"How do you figure?" His icy irises sparkle at my confidence.

"I don't lose." I shrug again, this time feeling a bit cocky.

"Babe..." His voice leaves him in a rasp as he leans in, his whiskey flavored breath warming my lips. "I've already won."

My breaths increase, my chest brushing his deliciously from the movements. I swear when he's near, I can feel everything. "How do you figure?" I copy him, licking my lips, wanting to close the distance between us, yet I hesitate.

He steps back, and I teeter to catch my balance. He reaches to the chair beside his door and lifts a leather jacket that's far too small to fit him. Stepping back from me, he twists the jacket around and stretches it, so I can easily read the patch on the back.

"For me?"

He nods, suddenly appearing a little nervous. Not like my alpha biker at all.

"No one's ever gotten me anything like this before," I admit. Bringing my hand up to his face, my thumb brushes over his lips. "This kinda makes it official, huh?"

He nods again. "I told you, I've already won."

"You would rather win me?"

"Of course. Nothing could ever compare," he replies quietly.

"Oh, biker..." I pull him to me, finally planting my mouth on his. I lose myself in the kiss, reveling in the knowledge that to him, nothing compares to me. That knowledge is consuming, knowing that you mean something to that extent to another.

He pulls away to set the jacket beside us, then strips me of my clothes. Leaving me in only my thong, he lifts the jacket again, and I slide my arms in the soft black leather. I've seen his jacket hanging up, and it's the same as mine, only much bigger.

His desire filled gaze flicks over me. "If I wouldn't end up killing someone, I'd tell you to stay like that forever." He rumbles. "I didn't think you could get any sexier until now."

His blazing stare has me feeling every bit of it too. He doesn't want some frilly lingerie, but a scrap of underwear and a jacket with his name on it. Men are so strange and yet easy to please. "You like your name on my back, cupcake?" I ask, coyly.

He straightens up and growls. There are no words involved. Just some primal sound that has him sounding more inhuman than the average male. With one hand he jerks me against his vast chest, my arms flying forward to hold onto him. His lips come back to mine, impatient and needy. His tongue thrusts inside as the fingers on his free hand push my panties aside, finding my pussy in a rush.

He's nearly frenzied like the first time he took me on the hood of my car. Two fingers fill my center, and I gasp into our kiss as he plunges them deeply into my core. He doesn't allow me to pull away either, owning every whimper and moan that tries to escape between our lips. His other massive hand grips my ass cheek, keeping me firmly against him.

His fingers pump, going in deep and quick until my climax thunders through me. The pleasure soaks my entrance from his touch alone. I never want him to stop this madness—

it's addicting. He coaxes my pleasure so easily, my body wanting to bend to his touch to please him.

His fingers leave me, and I'm so close to begging him to keep touching me. His fingertips rub over my stiff nipples drawing another moan from me. He pulls back, and I ask breathily, "What..." I trail off as he draws his fingers in his mouth next, sucking them clean. Soft pants leave me, witnessing him so savage when it comes to me is a huge turn on.

"I want to taste you when I fuck you, and it'll be even better if I'm sucking on your tits while I'm buried inside you." His free hand falls to my thigh, hiking it around his hip so he can sink his length in with one firm thrust.

"Oh, fuck," I moan as he fills me so completely. "Your cock...it's so fucking big...so good."

"Mmm, I love hearing that come from your mouth." His palm on my ass moves to my thigh to lift my other leg around his waist. When he has me completely wrapped around him, one hand palms my ass cheek while the other grips the back of my neck. I couldn't go anywhere even if I wanted to. This man and his big-ass muscles have me surrounded by him.

He kisses me deep and wild, his lips punishing my mouth as he takes more and more. This level of fucking is so powerful, so damn primal, I feel like we could bring down the clubhouse if he wished. He's deep enough that I could swallow and feel the tip of his cock in the back of my throat.

A cry bursts free from me and his mouth moves to my throat, his five o' clock shadow scratching along the way. The stubble against my skin burns in a delicious reminder that Mercenary is ravishing me. A few jerks of his hip, drawing moans from me isn't enough. He slams us to the bed. He rarely takes me on my back, but right now, he hikes my legs up farther, resting my ankles on his shoulders as he buries himself to the hilt.

I scream his name, and he revels in it. His gaze is full of possession and promises. I'm falling in love with this man. I know it. I can see it in the way he looks at me, how it hits me straight in my heart. I care for him.

His mouth moves lower, sucking and biting along the way until he pushes my breasts against each other. "I love tasting your pussy juice on your tits, straight fucking perfection."

They're big enough that my nipples nearly touch, and he sucks and laps at them with such unrestrained eagerness that I shoot off like a rocket again. My climax is so strong, my body feels like it's floating through space. He groans into my heated flesh as I cry out in bliss, my body shuddering with satisfaction.

His gravelly voice whispers my name over and over like a chant, and my insides squeeze his cock, rewarding his plea. "You taste so damn good. You smell so damn good. Fuck, I just can't get enough of you," he admits and sucks the top of my breast marking me in purple and maroon once again.

I'm not going to be the only one this time. My tongue whispers over his sweat slickened flesh, the salt is tangy and addictive. Reaching the middle, I breathe his scent in deeply, letting the leather and hint of cologne eclipse me like a heated blanket. This may be Texas, but I love it when he makes me burn when he makes me sweat.

My teeth clamp down, and his back stiffens in response. He's bitten me before, but this motherfucker is mine. It's time I claim him just the same. My tongue swirls the area, and I draw the flesh into my mouth until I've left a mark. I continue my task, peppering half a dozen hickeys over his neck. Releasing the skin, I breathe against his throat, claiming him with a ferocious purr, "Mine."

"Fucking right," he rasps and slams into me, pouring his come deep. The throbbing of his thick cock has me exploding all over his dick, gripping and releasing again and again. Both of our centers fight each other as we come together, skyrocketing with our pleasure. He kisses me once more, soundly, ending his passion perfectly. The man can fuck like no other.

Once we catch our breath, he climbs off me, holding a hand out to pull me to my feet. "I love the jacket, thank you."

He nods, tugging me toward the shower. "Good. I spoke to Princess before she ordered the patch. I told her you're always in tank tops." He heads for the bathroom, and I trail along.

"They're easier to work in, especially since it's so damn hot here most of the year."

"She figured. Said she's going to order you some with my patch on the back, so you always have my name on you."

"If it were anyone other than Princess, I'd be pissed over this."

He flips on the shower. "I know, babe. I'm glad you two hit it off, even if you burned half the shit she was cooking."

I burst out laughing. That was definitely one way for me to leave an impression on the queen of the club. She doesn't fuck around though, and I liked her instantly for it. He rids me of my jacket and underwear before tugging me into the water with him. His hands already stirring up my fire inside for another round.

Sapphire Knight

22. **Women who say "I want a bad boy"**
are clueless. What you need is a man who
will break someone's face for you but
also make you breakfast in bed.
- #ZKK

MERCENARY

Three days pass in no time, and before I can blink, we're pulling our bikes to a stop not far from one of the Fists' clubhouses. Odin remains on his motorcycle beside me. "Now we wait for the sign from Spider," he says, repeating the plan we've gone over each day, so everyone remains on track. His cobalt irises glance around at everyone minus Viking, the NOMADS, and Saint. Viking and the NOMADS are all with Spider, and Saint is driving the dump truck, on his way to us.

Odin speaks louder over the cars passing us on the highway. "When Spider blows the other club up, Ares' charter and ours will storm the Iron Fists clubs at the same time. That way it all happens at once, and there's less chance of reinforcements getting to other clubs to fuck us up. Saint will be right behind us. Half of you load up in the back, and everyone be ready to fuck shit up. The NOMADS and the Prez will be meeting up with us coming from the other direction."

Speaking of Saint, the beefy dump truck comes into view with his crazy ass hanging halfway out the window, flipping us the bird. The vehicle eventually pulls off the side of the road ten feet in front of us, and multiple kickstands hit the dirt. We're tucked right behind a group of bushes alongside the road. It'll be easy for us to get the hell out of here but also keep the waiting motorcycles hidden.

We decided that our bikes may be quicker and easier to hide if the cops show up. With a van, we risk a group of us getting popped and snatched up by the police. None of us want to have a shoot-out with the law or end up in jail. Another downfall of driving the van is if the Fists happen to muster up some backup, they could easily catch and kill us in one van.

Patting my chest, I reassure myself my vest is securely strapped on. I can feel the warmth but smoothing my fingers over it helps my mind catch on that shit's about to get real. We've spoken about it over the past few days, working out times and places, all the fine details, that sort of shit. This type of thing always seems surreal until it's actually happening.

Nightmare, Odin, and I remain on our bikes as Sinner, Blaze, Chaos, and Torch dismount. Blaze and Torch each take out a small glass vile filled with white powder and put it to their nostrils. Snorting up a deep inhale of powder, their eyes slam closed with the impact. A few beats pass as the drug hits them then they're all piling into the back of the massive truck.

I guess we all have our own ways of dealing with what's about to go down. Various brothers took a few shots of moonshine before we left as well. I, on the other hand, strapped on my bulletproof vest. I need to be clearheaded for this; I don't intend to die today.

The three of us riding are the biggest here other than the NOMADS, so it'll be easier if we approach the compound on our bikes. The smaller guys need more of the protection of the vehicle. Not saying they can't hold their own, but Nightmare, Odin, and I could probably take down a small army just the three of us. Viking tried to make Odin stay back in case anything happened to him. He'd need to step up as the new Prez, but O wasn't hearing it.

"Here we go." Odin blows out a breath, eyes trained to the sky.

"We've waited long enough," Nightmare growls and flicks open a purple switchblade. "I have a promise to keep."

An explosion rattles the ground, a smoke cloud rising toward the clouds, and the truck ahead of us lurches forward. The guys in the back are most likely holding on for dear life, so they don't show up with broken bones before the fight begins. Rocks spew in their wake and our engines thunder to life. The three of us move quickly to tuck in behind the brothers.

We get one chance to make our surprise entrance; it has to go off without a hitch. The other club will already be wondering what the hell's going on with the loud noise. With any luck, they'll think it was weather related, but I'm not holding my breath on that one. Our bikes lurch forward as we attempt to keep speed with Saint. The fucker has a lead foot, even in a heavy-ass truck.

I take up the rear. On a mission, we still don't break formation. I can't help but send up a prayer that God be on my side today. Chevelle's become too important to me. I don't want to leave her so quickly. I need more time in this life with her.

As we approach the electric chain-link fence, I brush the thoughts away. My mind chides myself for being a pussy. I need to harness my anger and get some payback for these assholes trying to hurt Chevy. I have to make it safer for her so she can do what she loves.

Hopefully the massive tires we stuck in the back of the truck work, and none of the brothers get toasted from the fence. Saint picks up more speed, and as we get closer, we fall back. Just in case the fence flies toward us with the impending impact, we don't want to be prematurely injured. My gaze skirts around the surroundings in the moments we have before shit hits the fan.

An Iron Fist attempts to leap out of the way but Saint slams on the gas, mowing the guy over and flying through the locked gate. We swerve around a bloody, detached leg and I decide right then to keep my eyes on the target and nowhere else. Some of the rival MC members out in the yard take off in different directions. Saint runs anyone over in his path.

Odin yanks a Glock from his boot, lacing the men still running away with bullets. They fall to the ground in motionless heaps. O doesn't even falter with the deaths, and I can't help but wonder what kind of life he had to make him so hard inside. He's too young to be so damn jaded. The kid's like nineteen. Regardless, he carries out orders, killing on sight.

This isn't payback. No, this is an extermination.

Viking said he only allows someone to fuck with him so much before he makes an example of them. He's setting the bar really fucking high, so bigger clubs won't attempt to fuck with us in the future. He said we knock out a huge, ruthless outlaw club and word will travel fast and far. One thing is for certain, this damn sure isn't Chicago. Texas is an entirely different type of beast.

Saint veers off to the side, the brothers spilling from the back. We pull to a stop on the other side of the truck for protection, weapons in hand as Viking and the NOMADS roar in from behind. They dismount their bikes beside us, so Odin and Spider can defend the vehicles and get anyone who may try to escape.

The brothers and NOMADS storm the club. Viking's first in, clad with an AK-47. He pops rounds off clearing a path through the men already shooting at us. Nightmare takes off past me toward a hallway. Exterminator's hot on his heels tossing smoke cans in his wake. The clubhouse is bigger than ours, with rooms and hallways veering off in every direction it seems.

I split off with Torch, having his back as he works to clear various rooms. We come across multiple bikers and return fire. Whores scream frantically, running in all directions. It's pure chaos; the magnitude of this job didn't fully hit me until now. No wonder the Iron Fists were able to keep coming at the Oath Keepers over the years. They're fucking everywhere!

We leave the whores be, as they're most likely not here of their own free will. The members we caught from The Pit were tortured extensively and admitted to all types of sordid shit going on at this club. The President, Puppet, has been around for far too long. He's had free reign from his high number of members and secret compounds spread from Texas to California.

Someone comes at me from behind, catching me off guard. A forearm wraps around my throat, and I rear back, stumbling backward until I slam him into the wall. It dazes him enough to shake his arm lose, and I spin around. He lands a blow to my jaw. Good thing the fucker's practically made of concrete; the hit against my jaw doesn't even rock me. He gets another in close to my temple, and I see red.

I counter with a right straight into his gut and then stun him with a head-butt to his nose. *Stupid motherfucker.* The bones crunch and blood pours free like a faucet. His arms flail, looking for purpose and I take a step back, with my left foot forward as I land a solid uppercut with my right. He wavers for a second then drops to our feet like a sack of flour. I land a kick to his temple for good measure.

"That's for sneaking up on me, motherfucker."

"Come on." Torch nods with an amused eyebrow lift. We keep to our path before a shrill whistle rings through the air. My gaze meets Torch's, and he holds a fist to his chest telling me to stay in place and remain quiet. He listens for a minute, then when a series of three sharp whistles follow, he nods for us to go back the way we came.

We make our way there quietly, waiting for any other clues. Back in the main entry, we're met with a scattering of dead bodies everywhere and Nightmare holding a bloodied older man. He's been beaten, and Night has the dark purple switchblade pressed firmly in place.

"Brothers," Viking thunders. "This is the root of our problems."

"Fuck off Oath scum," the broken man spits. Prez presses his finger into the man's temple so hard, I'm afraid he's going to stab through his skin and into the guy's brain. I have pent-up anger inside and enjoy a good ass kicking, but I'm not much for torture.

Blaze steps forward, his hunting knife in one hand and Glock in the other. The knife is already bloodied, I notice. "No, fuck you," he snarls and stabs Puppet in the gut. The older man hisses in pain but remains standing.

"I should've put a bullet in your skull," Puppet coughs.

In response, Nightmare flicks the blade up swiftly. He slices a gash into one side of Puppet's mouth. With that move, his eyes widen in shock from the jolt of pain.

Torch yanks his blade free from his holster, approaching Nightmare and the prisoner. He drives the blade into Puppet's upper thigh. "For Bronx, cunt."

The man groans, his head swaying side to side and I can't help but wonder how he's even still alive. Viking approaches them next, and I swallow roughly. He grabs the man's shirt collar with both hands and rips it completely open. Blood sops out from the gash Blaze already inflicted.

"For Scot—may our road father rest in peace—and for Princess, my ol' lady." He draws a small axe free, and with one harsh swing, hacks into the injury free side. That's the hit that hurts, as Puppet wails in pain.

Scowling, Nightmare growls, "The fun's only begun. When I'm finished with you, that hatchet will be child's play. You kidnapped my son, you beat my ol' lady, you *will* suffer."

With a nod to the brothers still beside me, I make my way outside before I puke my guts up.

23. Bikes are like ol' ladies, if it ain't yours don't touch!

CHEVELLE

Princess wears a pleased smirk as I tromp into the kitchen clad in leather. "Well, he was right about the fit, but you're not burning up in that jacket?"

"In here, no. The guys keep this place like an icebox." I gesture around at nothing in particular. "There's no way I can wear it outside though. Mercenary said you were ordering me some tanks also?"

She nods, opening the oven to pull a casserole out and check the temp in the middle.

"I appreciate it."

She waves me off. "It's nothing girl. I practically live in them too. You know how this summer heat gets the end of August."

"Miserable," I mutter, and she hums in agreement.

"So, what's up? The guys say you usually only cook when something's going on." We discussed this briefly the last time I was here too. I, in turn, burned her food, but not on purpose.

"What did Merc say before he left?"

"That he was going to help the club make it safer for me to be at The Pit."

"Did he tell you anything else?"

I shake my head. "No, and come to think of it, he distracted me before I could get anything else out of him."

"Sounds about right. Let's just say it has potential to be really dangerous. I'm trying to keep myself busy so I can pretend that they're fine and the cooking is keeping my mind occupied."

"But the cooking's really not?"

"No, not really."

"I get it; I can lose myself in an engine and drown any outside shit out."

"My best friend's out in the bar with Jude; they're getting drunk. That's her way of drowning it out."

"You don't want to be with them?"

"When my ol' man's on a run? No. We all cope differently. This is my way."

"That's Nightmare's ol' lady, right?"

"Yeah, Bethany. Their son's Maverick."

"I saw him running around the other day when Nightmare brought him to the club with him. Cute kid."

She smiles wide. "I know. I love that little boy as if he were my own."

"What about you and Viking?"

She wraps foil over the casserole and sets it aside on a hot pad. "What about us?"

"No kids for you guys?"

She places something else that resembles lasagna into the oven and turns to me. "Not yet."

I grow quiet, not sure what else there is to say about it. I don't want to push her on it. Usually, when you bring this stuff up, chicks chat your ear off. I keep to myself a lot besides when I'm in "Pit Master mode," so I'm not very good talking to women. They normally don't care for me much.

She leans against the counter across from where I stand and breaks the silence. "I have a feeling I'm going to be seeing a lot of you around here, Chevelle, so I'll share some back story with you."

"You do?"

Princess nods. "Mercenary did put his patch on you," she says, staring at me thoughtfully. I'm sure too many write her off as a pretty face and not realize she's wise beyond her years. "The club that the brothers went after beat me up badly when they stormed our compound. They did the same to Bethany as well and stole Maverick. The bastards nearly killed Blaze and succeeded in killing two of the other members."

My eyes widen. I knew they were dangerous, but goddamn, that is way beyond what I thought they were capable of. No wonder the Oath Keepers have been all over their asses when it comes to The Pit. "Holy shit," I whisper.

The skin around her eyes tightens as if she's remembering everything from that time. "That's not even everything. They hurt my father's old club too—the one Ares is President of now. They're with our guys now, helping. The Iron Fists club is massive, so the brothers had to sit back and wait for the perfect timing. I'm praying that they're right and that the time for retribution is now."

I swallow, my throat feeling dry with the sad story. "How do you deal with knowing about it all and having to stay here?"

"I deal because I couldn't imagine my life without Viking or the brothers of this club. They're my family, and they're doing what they feel is right, what will keep us safe. I'd do the same thing if I had the chance to offer them that protection."

She gestures to my leather jacket that I've worn since Mercenary left with the others. "You're a part of that family now too. We may not be in the club, but these men are my brothers. You're special enough to Mercenary for him to make you his ol' lady, and that makes you my sister."

"Thank you," leaves me on a breath and she flashes me a small smile.

"Now get your sexy ass on over here. I'm going to teach you how to make my mom's macaroni casserole. It's the best comfort food."

I hop off the stool and say a silent prayer that I don't ruin more of her food.

The thunderous roars outside from various motorcycles are loud enough to feel as if the compound is shaking from a small earthquake. The Oath Keepers all ride in together as one big group and park in front of the clubhouse. The tension in the air is thick. We wait with bated breath to see if they'll all return to us through that door. Anyone could've been injured or worse, killed. I may not know the other brothers like I do Mercenary, but I can only imagine how their loved ones feel, worrying about their men's safety.

The door to the main entry flies open and one after another, massive men enter. Their presence quickly fills up the space of the bar. The room's large but they almost make the area seem too small to fit them all at one time. Each one of them is splattered with blood, and one of the meanest looking guys of them all helps a smaller man through the door.

As soon as I find Mercenary, I jog to him. "What happened?" Thank God he's in one piece, and I don't think the blood he's wearing is his as most of it's dark from drying.

He glances at the two hobbling past us. "Exterminator's fine. Ruger was shot in the leg, so he's helping him."

"Shot? Shouldn't he be at a hospital?"

He shakes his head. "Nah, he'll be fine." The movement lets me catch the side of his face. A dark bruise is already forming near his temple.

"Shit, your face! Are you hurt badly?"

He pulls me into his arms, burying his face in the top of my hair. Princess did a good job of keeping me busy, but now that I have this big man in my arms, I realize just how worried I was for him. "I'm fine, I got jumped from behind. The fucker got a cheap shot in, catching me by surprise but I got the better of him."

Releasing a breath, I pull him to me, holding his muscular frame a bit tighter. Relief fills my chest as I take in his scent. "Thank God."

His fingers go under my chin, tipping my head up to meet his gaze. "Careful sweetie almost sounds like you care." His voice is gravelly, still laced with a dangerous edge. His body vibrates with adrenaline, and I know he needs to release some of it with me.

My bottom lip trembles and fuck if I don't want to kick my own ass for wearing my feelings so openly. It's been close to two months since he first showed up at The Pit demanding my attention. Now I don't want to think of a life without him in it. "I do care, cupcake; I'd miss kicking your ass at everything if something happened to you."

His lips turn up at the edges into an amused smirk and then *finally* his mouth falls to mine. With a swift kiss, he holds me firmly against him, warming me from within. "You remembered your jacket," he mutters when he eventually breaks free from my lips.

"Wouldn't forget it for the world," I admit softly, and he swallows.

"You make it really easy for a brother to fall for you, sassy-ass mouth and all."

"So charming." I roll my eyes, and his grin makes me smile in return.

"Tell me, Chevy. I want to hear you say it back."

Rather than correct him on my name, I give in and go a little further than his statement. With my mouth still close enough for my lips to brush his, I whisper, confessing the one thing I've never felt for another man. "I love you, Mercenary."

Mercs grin blooms into a full-blown, wide smile, white teeth showing and everything. He scoops me into his arms and my legs wrap around his waist to hold on. Embracing his neck, I press a quick peck on his lips, and he rasps, "I love you, Chevelle." Then he's walking us to the bar, joining his brothers in a shot to celebrate.

Whatever happened with the Iron Fists, it must've been a win for the Oath Keepers. While they celebrate together, I bask in the warmth of being wrapped in Mercenary's arms, knowing he loves me.

With a pleased gaze in my direction, he draws everyone's attention. "A toast! Here's to keeping our women and club safe. The Iron Fists breathe no longer, and we breathe easier without them."

"To our women," Viking echoes.

"The ol' ladies," Nightmare joins in.

"And to us," Saint interrupts. "Because God help anyone who attempts to take or hurt what belongs to us!" His stare locks on Sinner, and he nods his agreement.

"To kicking ass." Odin holds up his full shot glass.

"And family," I speak up. "With it, we have everything." I receive soft looks from the boulders of men and prideful glances from the woman beside them.

"Yes, we do," Mercenary mumbles in my ear. "With you, I have everything."

EPILOGUE

**If someone tells you that your car
doesn't need that much power,
stop talking to them. You don't need that
kind of negativity in your life.
- Pinterest Meme**

CHEVELLE

Twenty years later...

"Damn it, Chevelle, get her out of the driver's seat." Mercenary grumbles in my direction.

Nova giggles at her father's frustrated shout, and I smile wickedly. "Go ahead, Nova; crank her over before your daddy catches us."

"He's going to be so pissed. You heard him last week when he said my first car wouldn't be a race car."

I shrug. "Your father knows damn well that I do what I want to. Now let's hear how she purrs." I also remember when he swore Nova wouldn't go to prom either, yet she went to both her junior and senior proms. Or how he yelled the house down about her not being allowed to date, yet she did that too. He may huff and puff, but she has him wrapped around her finger.

I know what you're thinking, and no, we didn't teach her how to drive in a race car. Mercenary would've stroked out and spanked my pussy until I couldn't walk for a week if I had. However, with The Pit booming business wise, I had to treat my girl for her eighteenth birthday. I handed over the keys to my Chevy Nova, the car that her name originated from. Our daughter's about to graduate next month, and she's already been accepted into Baylor to study psychology, so she's earned it.

"That is *so* not fair, Daddy! Why does Nova get a car and I don't?" Our sixteen-year-old daughter shouts and runs to catch up with Merc as he storms in our direction.

My eyes meet Novas, excitement sparking in our matching irises. "Shit. Shelby's with Dad. You better drive this beast, baby girl."

With a calming breath, Nova puts the car into gear and then peels out as she slams on the gas.

Nova's definitely my daughter, one hundred percent. She doesn't get that lead foot from cupcake. Not that he's given me a chance to ever race him, the bastard. I think he's too chicken to get beat by his woman, but he swears it's because he doesn't want to see me lose to him. And we all know the stubborn man would never throw the race, even if it came to me. Not that I'd want him to. I'm perfectly capable of winning on my own.

"Where's Hemi?" I ask over the rumbling engine and stereo.

"Last I saw him he was talking to some girl on his cell."

I'm pretty certain Nova's twin brother's going to be hitting me up for a car next, or worse, asking Mercenary for a damn Harley.

"Who? Do you know her?"

She shrugs. "The last thing I want to overhear is his phone sex conversations."

"Ugh, Nova! That's my son!"

"He's my brother, I feel the same way." She makes a quick bleh face at me before concentrating on the road again.

Jesus, when did these kids grow up? I blinked, and they were no longer my babies but young adults.

We lasted two years before I threw the birth control out the window and demanded my stud give me a baby. The club was in a good place with possible enemies, and I had an abundance of his attention. I grew up alone nearly my entire youth. I wanted family and a lot of it.

What are the odds we'd get pregnant with twins on the first go? I was absolutely terrified when we found out. I had no parents, so how could I be a decent mother? Especially to two crying, pooping babies at the same time? Thankfully Mercenary's mother and father stepped in to offer advice and a compassionate ear to listen when we were feeling overwhelmed.

Being first time parents wasn't easy by any means but loving the twins and each other was effortless. Having Mercenary around all the time to demand random sex and spoil me, definitely helped get us through the rougher times. It seemed like once we finally caught our stride with the twins, that Shelby decided to surprise us. She's completely rotten too, every bit of the sixteen-year-old princess, but I'd have her no other way. I never had that freedom to be carefree, and I relish in seeing her so innocent and happy in life.

Hemi is another story all together. He's so much like his father it drives me crazy some days. I thought men grew into the broodiness, but hell no, that's not true. I have a broody-ass eighteen-year-old alpha who thinks he's God's gift to women. Hemi seems to believe that he has a chance with any female under the age of thirty, and cupcake eggs him on without a thought. Betty, Mercenary's mom, tells me that he was the exact same way at that age too.

And I'm in love—complete mind-blowing, soul shattering, heartwarming love with my ol' man. If I could go back and do it all over again, would I flip him like I did? Damn right. The stubborn biker needed to know he'd met his match, and I'm pretty sure that move hooked him from the start. He's been good to me all this time. I couldn't ask for a better man in my life. He loves me as if every day is his last and he's been a damn good father to our children.

With them, I'll grow old feeling loved, knowing what it is to love, and never be alone again.

MERCENARY

"I thought Nova wasn't getting a race car, Daddy?" Shelby's bottom lip trembles as she stares at me with a look like I killed a kitten.

"I had nothing to do with that." I point toward the car as we watch the ass end lurch forward with Nova driving like a maniac. "You know your mom does whatever she thinks is right."

Tears crest in her eyes and I swallow roughly. I don't do so well when my girls cry—any of them. Seeing them sad makes me feel like I've been stabbed in the chest. "But..." she whispers, trailing off as a tear breaks free, wetting her cheek as it runs down the creamy skin.

"What, baby? What is it?" I question softly and pull her to my chest where more of her tears break free.

"Mom always drives with Nova."

"Yeah? Why does that upset you so much?"

"Because she believes that Nova is so much like her."

"They have a lot in common, that's all." I attempt to reason as she hiccups.

"Nova's going off to college...but, *I'm* like mom."

"Well, you're all stubborn like your momma." A chuckle breaks free, as I think of my headstrong ol' lady.

"No, Dad," she pulls away, meeting my gaze with a new fire burning in her irises I've never seen before. "I want to race." She hisses and at that moment she's right, she's every bit Chevelle twenty years ago.

Sweet Jesus, I feel for the kid who falls in love with her. He'll have his hands full. Not that it'll happen before she's at least thirty.

"If you're serious, Shelby, I'll talk it over with your mom." I give in, not wanting her to be upset. I'd rather we know what she's doing versus her attempting to hide it from us. I'm an asshole to nearly everyone else, but one tear from my little girl and I'm bending over backward without blinking to make her happy.

She pops up, suddenly full of pep, and pecks my cheek. "Thanks, Daddy, love you!" And miraculously the tears instantly disappear, and she runs off toward the house.

Brat...she's spoiled like her mom! I wouldn't change them for the world though. I've never loved someone so much in my life.

HEMI

"Bro, you're not going to fuck her." My buddy Maverick chides through the phone. He's a couple years older than me, and he recently got his patch. His dad let him start prospecting for the Oath Keepers MC back when he turned eighteen. He thinks he's a total badass now because of it.

"I'm giving it two weeks at the most."

"Hmm, two weeks? You want to bet on it?"

"I've got fifty saying I hit it."

"All right, if it doesn't happen by the beginning of week three, you owe me fifty bucks."

"Done," I state firmly, knowing I'll wear her guard down by then.

He laughs. "You need to hurry up and come prospect for the club. The brothers would get in on this bet in a heartbeat and then you'd really lose some money."

I snort. "Because losing money should make me want to join up even faster?"

"No, because you'd have the entire club behind you. Think of the cash you'd get if you won."

"You have a point Mav; maybe I should talk to my dad about joining..."

THE END

Please let me know if you loved Chevelle and leave a review — even a few words, is amazing. Thank you for being a part of my world and until next time! XO- Sapphire

STAY UP TO DATE WITH SAPPHIRE

Email

authorsapphireknight@yahoo.com

Website

www.authorsapphireknight.com

Facebook

www.facebook.com/AuthorSapphireKnight

Made in the USA
Monee, IL
23 July 2021

74200913R00174